shattered

shattered

richard neely

VINTAGE CRIME / **BLACK LIZARD**

vintage books • a division of random house, inc. • new york

First Vintage Crime/Black Lizard Edition, March 1991

Library of Congress Cataloging-in-Publication Data

Neely, Richard.
Shattered / by Richard Neely. — 1st Vintage crime
Black Lizard ed.
p.   cm. — (Vintage crime/Black Lizard)
ISBN 0-679-73498-8 (pbk.)
I. Title.   II. Series: Vintage Crime/Black Lizard.
PS3564.E25P5   1991
813'.54—dc20   90-50635 CIP

Manufactured in the United States of America
10 9 8 7 6 5 4 3 2 1

shattered

The sound of the door opening triggered my release from the infernal dream, sent me spiraling up through smoke and flame and flying dirt and the roar of metal crashing through wood. I surfaced to consciousness in the usual position: on my back, right hand knuckled against the white headboard of the hospital bed, left hand pushed sweatily against my chest, heart thumping against the rib cage like a panicked bird.

I took a couple of deep breaths and blew them out slowly, fluttering the gauze that encircled my lips. I stared mindlessly at the pale green ceiling, a terrible apprehension gathering inside my stomach.

The bathroom door clunked open and closed, followed by a starched rustling sound and the shuffle of feet padding about the bureau. The same sounds heard every morning for the past seven months. Reality, stark and one-dimensional as a stage backdrop, slid into my mind.

"What time?" I said. It seemed too much of an effort to twist my head toward the chattering clock two feet

from my right ear. My shoulder was still stiff in the morning, although the cast had been removed weeks ago.

"Oh!" said Miss Dewar, startled. "I thought you were sleeping. It's seven fifteen."

She came and stood at the foot of the bed.

My eyes tunneled through the holes in the thick, mummifying bandages, absorbing the maternal smile that plumped up Miss Dewar's round pink cheeks.

"Well, Mr. Marriott, today's the big day."

The name still jarred. Marriott. After all the months of hearing it—from my wife Judith, from Dr. Stryker, from Miss Dewar, from the psychiatrist, Dr. Ragensburg—I was still unable to attach myself to it. For hours during the long sleeping-and-waking days I had repeated the name to myself, giving it dozens of inflections in the desperate hope that one of them would suddenly illuminate the man I had been. Nothing. It was merely a group of syllables that sparked a dog-like response. Marriott—Daniel Marriott. Oh yes, that's me. Here I am.

"Yes," I said to Miss Dewar, "the big day." The banality of the phrase, her phrase, brought a flicker of contempt, replaced immediately by shame. She had been good to me, kind and patient. Had the former Daniel Marriott been a cynical man?

Miss Dewar broadened her smile, patted the corner of the bed as if it were a part of me, and busied herself straightening up the room.

In fifteen minutes breakfast would be wheeled in. A light breakfast, I had been told. Tea and dry toast. There had been no need to explain the reason. The bandages

would be unfurled at eight o'clock. The shock of confronting my image might make me vomit. Still vivid was my reaction when the plaster cast completely encasing me had been cut away. Despite Dr. Stryker's strong objections, I had insisted on facing myself in a hand mirror. The reflection was not at all like a face. It was a grotesque, horrifying mass of swollen red-and-purple flesh, lashed together by angry welts. I had fainted.

The thought made my body shiver. It calmed as I recalled Dr. Stryker's expression the afternoon before, when he announced this morning's unveiling. His wide, thin mouth had curved into a smile of proud anticipation, as if he were a sculptor about to exhibit a masterwork.

Would Stryker's pride be justified? I twisted to my side (the left leg, which had been broken below the knee, gave a pins-and-needles tingle) and stared at the matching joined picture frames on the wheeled table. My eyes brushed across the image of Judith, noting the dark intensity of her eyes that seemed in conflict with her smile of supreme serenity, and fixed on the face of the man I had been. It was easy to judge it with complete detachment. A good looking face, with a strong bone structure, short straight nose, soft eyes, thick black hair unstreaked, as it was now, with gray. The portrait was an old one, taken when I was thirty. I was now thirty-eight. The face remained that of a stranger, no more familiar than a portrait seen when passing a photographer's show window. It should not be difficult to learn to live with it. But supposing, despite the surgeon's skill and the harrowing months of torture, the result was something monstrous?

Well, in that case, I would simply have to learn to live inside a monster. Inexplicably I sensed that in the life that was now a void I had been an adaptable man. And perhaps a vain one, judging by my refusal to permit Judith to attend the unveiling. Or was I of a considerate nature, concerned only with protecting my wife's sensibilities? I had no way of knowing, there were no remembered experiences to provide such insights into my character.

I noted, as usual, the inscription—"To Judie with deepest love"—then shifted my eyes to the clock. Seven-thirty. Some three hundred miles north, Judith should just be leaving our home in Kentwood to drive across the Golden Gate Bridge and down the Peninsula to the San Francisco airport. She would have breakfast in the terminal and board the nine o'clock flight to Santa Barbara, where she would rent a car and drive through the hills to the clinic. Promptly at ten-fifteen she would be walking through that door, her manner solicitous but with an undercurrent of gaiety, the latter not quite authentic. The routine had not varied in the seven months I had been at the clinic. Three times a week Judith arrived at mid-morning, stayed for lunch and left in mid-afternoon. Today there would be one electrifying change—when Judith left the clinic, I would go with her. If my face was still too frightfully distorted, I would insist that it be re-bandaged before she arrived. But go, by God, I would. I had to. I was ready to climb the walls.

Miss Dewar raised the venetian blinds on the large windows flanking the bed, and oblongs of late-July sun flashed across the polished floor. She left, cooing reassurances, to be replaced by a white-clad male attendant bearing a tray with the expected tea and dry toast, and the morning newspaper. I nibbled indifferently at the toast but gulped the tea to soothe my constricted throat. Swallowing, I still felt a soreness where the windpipe had suffered a splintered fracture. Judith had told me that it gave my voice a soft, husky quality. "Very distinctive," she said, smiling. "And really quite pleasant." To me, it sounded more like gravel'poured down a galvanized pipe.

However well intended, observations like that were among the more unsettling aspects of Judith's visits, emphasizing that we were in fact strangers. Perhaps not quite strangers. Something about the heart-shaped face framed with black, shoulder-length hair aroused a vague recognition, as one sometimes feels a subtle association with a picture in a magazine. But our attitudes toward each other were to me a complete blank, an ignorance that precluded expression of any intimate thoughts. Judith was a fine looking, almost beautiful woman of about my age (for some reason I couldn't bring myself to ask) and as my recovery progressed, I began to feel a physical need of her. A clue to that side of our marriage had first been provided weeks ago. As she rose from her chair to leave, I involuntarily clutched her hand, feeling a sudden overwhelming desire for human contact. Swiftly she bent down and kissed my palm, then my throat. Releasing her hand, she brought it down and gently stroked my loins. If there had been a lock on the door, I was damned sure I would have insisted she turn it and spring naked into the high hospital bed. (So I must have been an impulsive man, too.)

Softly she had said, "Soon, Dan, soon" and in a moment was gone. Each visit since had ended with similar gestures and a breathlessly spoken promise. Along with my rising anticipation, I was becoming anxious about what would be expected of me. I sensed we had been passionate in bed, and for hours after she had gone I would fantasize over the forms our pleasure may have taken. But I never spoke of it.

Time enough for that when we were alone together in the beach house Judith had rented south of Los Angeles. We would stay there for a few weeks, perhaps a month. A way station, she had said, to ease the return to normal life in Kentwood. Like bringing a deep-sea diver to the surface, I thought—slowly, to prevent the bends. More accurately, to toughen me up before returning to the scene where both physical and mental identity had been lost.

Again and again, at the urging of Dr. Ragensburg, a psychiatrist affiliated with the clinic, she had recounted the events of that horrifying night; morning really—two-thirty A.M. January first. Far from sober, we were returning from a New Year's Eve party at the home of our best friends, Ginnie and Jeb Scott. Through the fog a soft rain was falling as I guided the car up the road climbing the mountain that was the scenic pride of the county. A thousand feet up, less than a mile from our home, we spun across an oil slick. The wheel jerked from my hand. There was a sickening skid and the car plunged off the road. Judith was thrown out almost immediately, suffering only abrasions. I was trapped inside—unconscious, probably from my head striking the steering column—as the car careened and flipped over and over five hundred feet down, smashing to a stop against a thick oak, half toppling it. Somehow Judith managed to scramble down the mountainside and drag me from the wreckage. She ripped off her slip, wetting it in the rain, and swabbed at the blood pouring from my pulped, broken face. We were completely isolated, our own empty house the only one within miles. The road above was lightly travelled even in daylight and patrolled infrequently by the police. Accepting her only choice, she left me, stumbled and clawed her way frantically up to the road, hiked to our house and called the police. Barely alive, I was hauled up the mountainside on a litter. Every bone and cartilage in my face had been crushed, eight teeth knocked out, trachea splintered, right shoulder, arm and hand broken, four ribs and left leg fractured, spleen ripped. My survival was considered a medical phenomenon.

After two weeks in the intensive care unit of the Kentwood Hospital, mute, immobile and amnesic, I was transported by ambulance to the clinic tucked in the sunburned hills back of Santa Barbara, three hundred miles to the south. The move was necessary in order to employ the services of the West's foremost plastic surgeon, Dr. Vincent Stryker ("a miracle worker," one of the leading news magazines had called him).

The weeks that followed told me one thing about myself—I had a high tolerance for protracted pain. Bone from my intact right leg and skin from my abdominal wall—"donor areas," the doctor called them—were borrowed to structure and package the face. Cartilage from my left wrist was transferred to form a nose (for three weeks the wrist had been fastened to the center of my face to ensure a viable graft). A dental surgeon had anchored new teeth to those that remained. (Oddly, lips and gums had sustained only minor damage.) Finally, immobilized in hard plaster, left leg suspended in air, right arm jackknifed above my chest, I remained rigidly on my back, alone in a vast mental vacuum filled only at night by a holocaust of dreams. Often, as now, I wondered if the dreams—centered always on tumbling, fiery, earth-spewn images—were evoked by Judith's repeated accounts of the accident; or did they sneak out at night from the subconscious jail that imprisoned the true experience?

At my urging, my loss of memory was explained by Dr. Ragensburg, a short, portly man who looked more like a bespectacled druggist than a psychiatrist. Sitting at my bedside, hands laced across his melon of a stomach, he spoke as a lecturer forced to address an audience of laymen, and thus dubious of being understood.

"The crash itself, the injuries you sustained—these only partially explain your amnesia. There was no brain damage. True, you suffered concussive trauma. But this usually produces only a loss of *recent* memories—retrograde amnesia, we call it; you would probably recall events that occurred some time ago. In your case—the so-called fugue state—you have forgotten not only your identity, your occupation, your age, your address, you even fail to recognize your wife of some sixteen years." He gave a melancholy twist of his mouth. "It is the typical paradox. All memory is gone, yet your basic habit patterns remain unimpaired. You can talk, write, reason; in fact, you are quite normal aside from the amnesia."

"If the head injuries didn't cause it, what did?"

"Oh, the head injuries doubtless contributed. But, as I say, probably only partially. No, the root cause, I believe, is psychogenic. The *material* of memory is still there, but you have repressed it below the level of consciousness. You unconsciously censored the material because it is too distressing to be borne."

I looked at him skeptically. "You mean I *want* to forget the life I lived before the accident?"

"Either the life you lived or a specific intolerable situation—some emotional shock which amounted to a crisis in your life."

I could not believe him. It all sounded like so much psychoanalytic mumbo-jumbo.

"Is it possible to say how long the loss of memory will last?"

He pursed his lips. His eyelids dropped behind the thick lenses. "I don't wish to depress you, Mr. Marriott. Nor do I wish you to face the future with pessimism. "But"—he waggled a finger—"you are a man of strong character, I think. It is better, perhaps, that you know the truth, at least as much as we are aware of it." He paused. "Clinical records are filled with cases of individuals who have forgotten their personal histories for periods of many years. From what I have observed, your memory blockage is of massive proportions. We have tried free association, drugs, hypnosis—all proved methods for cure. In your case, all have failed to release the lost material. Now, it

may be that when you return home and revisit familiar
scenes, when you are faced once more with circumstances
associated with the trauma, you may show a remarkable
recovery. But I ask you not to depend on it."

A withering thought struck me. "Is it possible that the
amnesia could be permanent?"

His head bowed. "It is possible."

I swallowed, striving to contain a wave of terror.

"Does my wife know all this?"

"I felt it my duty to tell her."

Now, shaking off the somber thoughts, I picked up the
morning paper. I glanced idly at the headlines, then automatically removed the last section and turned to the
business pages. The procedure appeared to be an in-
grained habit, obviously carried over from my other life.
I had been a stockbroker, partner of my closest friend,
Jeb Scott, in the firm of Scott & Marriott on Montgomery
Street, San Francisco. I noted that the market was staging
a summer rally, the Dow-Jones for the previous day gain-
ing eight points on volume of eleven million shares. I studied a number of listings, understanding the corporate
symbols but failing in the usual attempt to interpret them
in terms of value or performance. It was like knowing a
house only by its facade, not by its inhabitants or furnish-
ings. I had experienced a similar reaction on the three
occasions Jeb Scott came to visit: Jeb's Wall Street verbi-
age—delivered like the incantations of a cultist bent on
reclaiming a defector—conveyed little more meaning than
a laundry list. Jeb had seemed surprisingly disappointed
that talk of business failed to restore my memory.

Ginnie Scott, Jeb's wife, had been more penetrating, although not with words. She had come down with Judith only once, some weeks after I entered the clinic. Sitting primly beside the bed, she had spoken very little, her brown eyes regarding with empathy the apertures in my entombed head. Then, with no warning expression, Ginnie's face fell into her hands and she wept long and quietly. I had the feeling she was stricken with remorse, torn by the thought that if it had not been for her New Year's Eve party this awful thing would not have happened. She had written a note apologizing for her outburst. She would not, she said, visit me again unless there was something helpful she could do; her presence, she feared, only contributed to my discomfort. More likely to *her* discomfort, I had thought, remembering that vulnerable face.

The door swung open and Dr. Stryker's long, white-coated figure stood framed there for a moment. His bony, freckled face was sharp with interest.

I felt myself stiffen, dread churning up to my throat.

"Good morning, Mr. Marriott. We're ready now."

Dr. Stryker's small consulting room was lit only by splinters of light filtering through closed venetian blinds. I sat with my back to the window in a black leather chair, skull embraced by a winglike head rest. Miss Dewar stood lumpily erect off to the right. Dr. Stryker, slightly in front of me.

I closed my eyes.

The snip of the shears was loud in my left ear. I heard them clink as they were set down on the table next to the black examination couch. I felt a slight tug near my temple, heard the abrasive whisper of gauze as the doctor began gently to unwind it. It was as though a heavy load was being lifted from my face, the skin becoming more sentient with each unwinding.

Abruptly my face was struck by what seemed to be a great rush of air. The bandages were off.

My eyes opened and blinked into a pencil-thin shaft of light. Behind it, Dr. Stryker's body loomed like a giant, angular shadow. The tips of his fingers slid like dry little cushions across my forehead, down the nose and cheeks, along the jawbone.

"Move your face, Mr. Marriott. Grimace."

I grimaced, cautiously. My heart twitched. My face felt like one big chapped lip about to crack apart.

"Good," the doctor said. "The keloids have definitely been eliminated. There will be no contracture, no deformity." The light snapped off. "Will you please open the blinds, Miss Dewar."

Behind me, the louvers rattled open. Daylight crashed into the room, reflecting from the wall near the door. Squinting, I saw that Dr. Stryker held a round hand mirror. He handed it to me.

"Don't expect perfection, Mr. Marriott."

For a moment, teeth clenched, I held the mirror against my chest. Then I slowly raised it to my face.

This time I was tensed against shock, only to find that my first reaction was one of agreeable surprise. My immediate throught was, he's given me back my face! Or at least it was a reasonably accurate facsimile of my photograph. But it looked pasted together, as if the victim of a bizarre practical joke. The variegated flesh ranged from flour-white to pink to scarlet, striated with hair-thin red scars.

"The swelling is entirely gone. Mr. Marriott. The discoloration, the patchwork appearance, will disappear. The scars between the grafts will become virtually unnoticeable. You will look practically normal."

I heard the doctor as if from a great distance. I was looking deeply into my own reflected eyes.

A shallow breath whistled from my throat. I seemed to be looking at a man I knew with startling intimacy but was unable to place. A fragmented memory began to form. For a split instant the pieces darted together like metal fittings homing to a magnet. Then they fell apart. But not before my senses had absorbed the blurred image of an unidentifiable woman around whom drifted an aura of death.

2

The cottage at San Clemente sat on high dunes, the plank deck joined to the beach by a dozen wooden stairs. Inside, two bedrooms adjoined a long glass-fronted living room separated from a small kitchen by a service counter.

Immediately upon entering. I pulled the curtains against the savage late-afternoon sun that seemed to scream into my naked face. Perched on a counter stool and sipping a beer from the well-stocked refrigerator, I kept my face turned to the wall even though Judith was in the bedroom emptying the two large suitcases. Hidden so long behind bandages, I now felt guilty of indecent exposure. All during the more than two hour ride south, even through the trembling heat and smog of Los Angeles, I skulked low in the passenger seat, chin sunk deep in the turned-up collar of a new sport coat. Certainly I couldn't blame Judith for this morbid self-effacement. Except for a quick, uncertain flicker in her eyes when first confronting me in the darkened hospital room, she had given no sign of repugnance. Quite the contrary. Without making me feel on exhibition, she had nevertheless marvelled at the facial reconstruction. "Just a little while in the sun, Dan," she smilingly reassured me, "and you'll be ready for Hollywood." Easy on the sun, warned Dr. Stryker; only a few minutes a day in the beginning, face protected by a special healing ointment.

Judith had surprised me by driving down in a new white Thunderbird convertible, the replacement for the car that had been destroyed. She brought me a new, though minimal wardrobe, tailored to measurements taken some weeks before; necessary because I had lost weight since the accident. Expendable weight, I was glad to notice. During the drive down from Santa Barbara, conversation had been sporadic and one-sided, Judith breaking the long silences with expressions of delight at my release and hints of intimate pleasures awaiting us at the beach cottage. Concerning these pleasures she seemed archly non-specific, as if to incite my own ideas on the subject. The only idea I had—the conventionally-positioned union of man and woman—induced, not desire, but a deepening depression. Not because I was unaware of my own sexual role—instinct, it was evident, had its own memory—but because I was ignorant of exactly how that role was to be projected. Would we mutely join together like virginal newlyweds under the sheets in a dark room? Would we first, fully-clothed and lounging on a sofa, rise to passion on a wave of kisses? The thought was frightening. My scarred, patched face was not yet ready for intimate contact (I had averted it when I stood to greet her in the hospital room and she rushed to embrace me). Perhaps for a day or two she would

17

expect no love-making, at least until, in conversation, we had explored our previous attitudes. The thought brought a feeling of temporary relief.

Now, gripping the cold can of beer, I got up nervously from the counter stool and walked to the windows. Gingerly I raised a corner of the green curtain and peeked out. I blinked, adjusting my eyes, bringing into focus the shoreline a couple of hundred feet beyond a stretch of uninhabited white sand. Off to the left stood a sun-bleached board fence, perhaps eight feet high, extending to the waterline where it was anchored to huge rocks. About thirty yards to the right stood a matching fence. As Judith had suggestively promised, it was a completely private beach. I looked straight ahead, beyond the rolling breakers to the fat red sun approaching the horizon. I glanced at my watch. Ten to five. "Cocktails at five," Judith had said as though suggesting an assignation. I gave my head a shake and dropped the curtain. Feeling suddenly claustrophobic, I moved to the door, flung it open and stepped outside.

The deck, jutting more than a dozen feet from the house, contained two director's chairs and two divans lying flat. For some reason the divans caught my interest. The frames were highly polished, heavy dark wood, cushioned with deep blue pads of stout canvas. A memory stirred and the word Mexico dropped into my mind. Then, Acapulco. The name aroused no association but stuck in my barren brain like a direction sign. I sat on the edge of a divan, rubbing a hand over its coarsely padded surface, breathing deeply to relax, and let the word Acapulco float about freely. I must not concentrate on it; that would only insulate it against meaning. *Puerto Vallarta*. There! Acapulco had attached itself to Puerto Vallarta and was instantly absorbed by it. Images sprang up. A small Mexican seacoast town, houses stacked on a green hill. Great combers thundering to the beach. A swimming pool—shallow, not more than three feet deep—roaming in an odd geometric pattern beneath low-hanging tropical trees. And surrounding the pool, lined up in neat rows—divans. Each identical to the one on which I now sat. There was a woman, stretched out, naked to the waist, in the soft darkness. She was fumbling with the strings that bound her bikini bottoms. "Now!" she whispered tensely. *"It's got to be now!"*

"Anyone for a quick swim?" Judith said behind me. "It'll put a nice edge on the drinks."

Startled, I turned my back to the sun and shielded my face with a hand. She stood in the doorway poised and smiling, jet-black hair carefully combed and shimmering down to the white ruff collar of a lacy beach jacket. Through it I could see her lithe body, ruddy from the sun, breasts and loins scarcely covered by thin strips of hot-pink cloth.

Diffidently I said, "It's a little late in the day. Perhaps tomorrow."

Her eyes, dark as obsidian, glazed over. Turning, I saw that the sun was dropping behind the sea. In a few minutes the protective twilight would arrive. Still shading my face, I smiled up at her, gathering the courage to say,

"Well, why not. I've got to expose this lily-white body some time."

In the bedroom, pulling on dark-red trunks, I reflected on the clouded memory evoked by the name Puerto Vallarta. Perhaps it was not memory at all. At the clinic, Judith had described our trip to Mexico the previous fall. Mexico City, Acapulco, Puerto Vallarta (where the Scotts had joined us). Most likely she had mentioned the divans and the oddly-shaped pool under the trees. But I was certain she had not spoken of the seductive scene on the divan. Pure fantasy, I decided, the libidinous imaginings of a deprived male. Anxiety nudged at my innards as I quickly pulled on a terrycloth robe (white, I thought, as the body) and went outside.

She stood spread-legged at the waterline, beach jacket heaped behind her on the sand, waving me to hurry. As I trotted down the stairs and plodded across the hot sand, she galloped into the surf and sprang out in a flat dive under an oncoming wave. Up she bobbed, capless, hair seal-slick, laughing and gesturing me forward. I waited until she dived again, then flung aside the robe and raced to clothe my waxen body in the water. A wave smashed above my knees, sent me reeling back, feet frantically seeking anchorage in the swirling sand. I gritted my teeth, staggered forward, measured a breaker and dived through it, straight and clean and with complete muscular control. Shooting out into the trough, I suddenly felt a wild elation. Turning my head, I saw Judith watching with a look of eager anticipation. I grinned, then laughed. Her answering laughter was wild, almost drunken. Together we knifed through the next wave, then stood side by side facing the shore, waiting for a big one. When it came it was a bulging, towering, black-green monster. Bodies stretched out rigid, we caught it at the crest and rode it breathlessly until, as our bellies grazed the sand, it spent itself in rolling foam.

I lay on wet, packed sand, gazing at the purple horizon, enjoying a wonderful exhaustion. She went to her beach jacket, returning with two lit cigarettes. Handing me one, she sat down and hugged her round knees, staring into my face with a small intent smile. Now I felt no embarrassment, no necessity to hide. The pounding of the waves, the shared exhilaration, had at last taken me out of myself. For the first time in memory I felt free. I closed my eyes.

The mouth that closed on mine was soft but insistent, parted lips brushed with the salt and dampness of the sea. My eyes popped open and as quickly squeezed shut. My hand released the cigarette, jerked up as if to ward her off but remained on her smooth shoulder, slowly squeezing it. She reached back and fussed for a moment with the narrow top of her bikini. The strip of hot-pink cloth snapped away, drifting to the sand. Hand behind my head, she drew my face up to crush it gently against her taut breasts. I heard her breath whisper, "Oh, my darling, my darling," felt her hand slither down my body.

I wrenched away, feeling an inner congealment. Fear? I looked into eyes that were suddenly remote.

Perhaps I was merely rejecting the role of passive male. Words faltering, I said, "I don't know . . . who we were."

Her eyes softened and a smile played at the corner of her mouth. She looked out to the flat ocean painted red by the departing sun. "Let's say we were lovers," she said evasively.

She turned back to me. I looked at her narrowly, trying to fathom the unknown in her. As if to sharpen my insight, she widened her eyes into innocent circles. Unenlightened, I shook my head and turned away, my mind fixing on the only evident truth—a strange, virtually naked woman and an amnesic man with a seamed face and a body like tallow. I stood up self-consciously and wrapped myself in the terrycloth robe.

"Lovers," I repeated as she resignedly slipped on her sheer beach jacket. "After sixteen years of marriage? We seem to have beaten the averages." I was surprised to find myself using a stock market phrase.

With a trace of mockery, she said, "As you may have noticed, I'm eager to show you the complete portfolio."

At the house, we took turns showering, Judith first. After mine, I slipped back into the robe and came out on the deck to find her, clad in a scarlet dressing gown, lounging on a raised divan and sipping a martini. A pitcher of them sat on a low redwood table alongside her. I sat down on the matching divan, experiencing again a vague reminiscence, and poured a martini. Sipping it brought a small shock of recognition; it had been made, I knew, exactly as I like it—bone-dry and stinging cold.

"Another talent," I said, smiling into the glass.

"We hardly sampled the first one."

She would not let it alone. She seemed to be goading me, challenging my manhood. I finished the drink in a gulp, got up and swung around the table, looking down at her in the warm dusk. The whites of her eyes flashed up to mine. She twisted her body sideways, making room. I sat down. Instantly her mouth came up to mine. I grasped her shoulders and pushed her back, disconcerted at her insistence that she be the aggressor. Undaunted, she slid her hand beneath my robe, resolving affirmatively any question of manhood. Again I stood up, urged by a need to be on my own territory. She came up with me, still clinging, and wordlessly we drifted to the other divan that lay flat. Standing, she flung out of her robe, unfastened mine and pulled it from my shoulders, dropping it to the deck. She pushed me down until I lay supine, and explored my body with warm-breathed kisses. I slipped my hands under her arms and closed hard on her breasts, pulling her back on my chest. But she would not yield the initiative. She wriggled abrasively from my grip and skipped her mouth with slow emphasis down my chest, down my taut belly. I gasped as she enveloped the pulsating tumescence that now achingly demanded release. I reached for her shoulders to hoist her to me, to contribute to the foreplay and balance our passion. But at the touch, she came up fast, bestriding my hips. Expertly she guided the penetration. Then she laced her hands behind her neck, swelling her breasts, forcing her body into rhythmic muscular movement as she supplicated me to completion with blunt, prurient words harshly spoken.

Only after I was lost to the long spasm of ejaculation did I guess that she was experiencing sensory response.

As I surfaced, her cheek now pressed to mine, her body arched and still in the dominant position, I thought: *It was like this at Puerto Vallarta*. The thought brought a tingle of alarm.

She whispered, *"Now* do you remember?"

I felt gutted and alone. *"Part* of me remembers," I said, and realized my tactlessness.

She rolled away, rising to a sitting position.

I hiked myself up, watching her face in the flame of a match as she lit two cigarettes. She handed me one and I took a long drag.

"I mean does your *mind* remember?" Her voice probed like that of the psychiatrist at the clinic.

"I don't know. It may have been just a dream. A shallow pool under some trees. A divan like this . . ."

She gripped my knee. "It's not a dream. It *was* like this. We were in Puerto Vallarta. You were so . . . so uncooperative. And I was shameless." She started to say more, then stopped, as if awaiting my reply.

The admission gave me a sudden confidence. "You mean you . . ."

"I raped you," she said impatiently. "I couldn't wait for *you.*"

I was puzzled but not shocked. "Did you say, 'Now. It's got to be *now!'?*"

"Probably." She seemed to choose her words carefully. "There wasn't much time. It was our last night. We were leaving the next morning."

"But weren't we at a hotel? Wasn't there a bed?"

She stubbed out her cigarette, looking at me curiously.

"Yes, there was a bed. Twin beds. Just as in Acapulco. But you never shared mine."

I was startled. "You mean we weren't living as"—I resisted the stilted euphemism "man and wife" and sub-stituted—"we weren't lovers?"

She seemed to consider the word. "In a way, perhaps, we were lovers. But not really, not for a long time. Much too long."

Was that why we had gone to Mexico? To seek an end to sexual estrangement? To use the scented tropical nights as an aphrodisiac? I was struck by a chilling thought.

"Was there something wrong with me? Before?"

Her teeth flashed white. "You were quite capable, dar-ling."

"Then why—?"

"Let's not rush it, Dan. A little at a time. Let's just enjoy the way we are now."

Reluctantly I agreed, wondering at her obvious relief.

At two o'clock the next morning, unable to sleep, I stood at the bedroom window smoking a cigarette and staring out at the moonwashed beach. Tossing in bed, my mind had whirled with conjectures. It seemed apparent from Judith's attitude that she had been dominant in the marriage. Had I been one of those spineless idiots forever truckling to their demanding wives? Had business so preoccupied me that I had lost authority by default? Or had our sixteen-year marriage simply succumbed to indifference, prompting Judith to seek a revival of interest by reversing our marital roles? Somehow none of the conjectures seemed to fit.

Whatever the cause, I knew I could not endure remaining the passive partner.

I heard the soft twang of a bedspring, the striking of a match. Turning, I saw the glow of a cigarette, making luminous crescents of her half-closed eyes. I went and stood over her. She was covered only by a sheet tucked loosely under her arms, moonlight gleaming on her shoulders. I reached down, took her cigarette and ground it out in the ash try with my own. I grasped the top of the sheet and stripped it from her body. She started to rise but I pushed her roughly back. She lay there, not moving, watching intently as I sat down beside her. My hands moved over her, exploring, experimenting, as if I had unexpectedly come into possession of some new and fascinating adult toy. She reached for me but I pushed away her hand. Not until her body squirmed in pleading invitation and her breathing rose to gasping pitch did I allow her to touch me. Then I mounted her and brought her to clawing climax in a long, plunging union, she wildly lost in sensation, I rigidly controlled, timing the release for the climactic moment.

Afterwards, she lay next to me, tucking her head into my shoulder and expelling exhausted squeaks of pleasure. Her hands stroked me as if in humble gratitude. I now knew that earlier, on the divan, she had been challenging my memory, for some reason testing me. This time she had got what she wanted from the beginning.

3

On our first morning back in Kentwood, I drove to the scene of the accident. I located the point of final impact at the break in the toppled oak, the splintered raw wood now weathered gray. Crisp, brown leaves from the dead branches covered the parched ground, crackling under my feet as I stepped closer to examine the crusty bark on each side of the break. Deep scars and gouges testified that the car had struck with enormous force.

Looking back, my eyes travelled the route of the sheer descent. Five hundred feet almost straight down, through a density of scrub oak and seedling pines and coarse weeds, whose regrowth in the shale-laden earth now covered any trace left by the careening car. My gaze paused just below the road. It must have been there that Judith was flung out. I looked upward to where heavy foliage screened the lip of the road, marked only by the glint of sun striking the red hood of my parked sports car. Beyond, I followed the contours of the green-spiked hills folding into each other as they ascended. Above them, rising three thousand feet into the sapphire sky stood The

Mountain. "Sleeping Maiden" the Indians had called it—aptly, because it resembled nothing so much as a long, graceful woman lying supine, the summit a recumbent head joined to an escarpment that rounded into a breast and flowed down into a long flat belly.

Only that morning, Judith had suggested a drive to the mountaintop after breakfast. But I had been too intent on returning to where I now stood, although I had not said as much. For some reason, perhaps the wish to spare her a reprise of that agonizing night, I preferred to come without Judith. So I made the excuse that I wished to take the Porsche and drive about alone, "to see how much is familiar, without any coaching. Maybe it will help me remember other things." Judith had given me a long, wondering look but had not objected. Leaving her on the flagstone terrace where we had breakfasted, I had gone to our room, donned the dark-blue sports suit and gray slacks bought at San Clemente and, in an eagerness to be away, hurried to the garage without saying goodbye. Backing down the steep driveway to the road that snaked up the mountainside, I automatically pointed the car toward the valley floor. I knew, without thinking, precisely where the disaster had occurred. The night before, approaching our house in the dark after eight hours on the road from San Clemente, Judith had just rounded a curve when my stomach gave a twitch. Without a word from her—although I noticed her hands clench white-knuckled on the wheel—I knew we were passing the site of my undoing. A few minutes later, we were home.

The house, half hidden from the road below by a hedge

of pyracantha, sat on a broad shelf bulldozed out of the mountainside. A heavy shake roof covered the two stories, fronted with glass to capture the magnificent view of the valley and the Bay beyond. To the left of the house, surrounded by small islands of tropical landscaping dotting a flagstone terrace, was a forty-foot, rectangular swimming pool. After I hauled in the baggage and Judith led me through the large, expensively furnished living areas, I sat for a few minutes on the sofa trying to identify with my surroundings. Suddenly I felt jittery and jumped up immediately when Judith suggested we go to bed.

The upstairs consisted of three bedrooms and two baths. Judith had not offered to show me around, heading directly for the master bedroom at the front of the house. Entering the large, square room, I was struck with surprise. From the satin-covered bed to the silken draperies, from the quilted chaise to the cosmetic-strewn dressing table, the room was utterly feminine. I had the impression that no man had ever so much as crossed the threshold.

I made no comment, but when she went into the adjoining bathroom and turned on the shower, I slipped down the hall to explore. Starting at the rear of the house, I opened the door on what was presumably a guest room. Giving it no more than a glance, I headed back, past a bathroom, to the door next to the master bedroom. The door was locked. I stood there for a minute staring curiously at the knob. Then the pipes shuddered as the shower was turned off and I returned swiftly to the master bedroom. *Her* room.

Later, alone in the bathroom brushing my teeth, I

glanced next to the shower stall and saw another door. Going to it, I turned the knob. Locked. A question that had been sitting quietly in my mind now spoke. Had I occupied the room behind the locked door? At one time, the connecting door to the bathroom must have been unlocked. Could something have happened to provoke one of us to seal the other off? Had it been done after the accident or before?

My mind echoed her remark made on the divan that first night at San Clemente: "Yes, there was a bed. Twin beds. But you never shared mine." Occasionally I pondered those words during our stay at the beach house, finally dismissing them as applying only to our brief sojourn in the hotel in Puerto Vallarta, where, I decided, we had become temporarily alienated by some petty wrangle. Now the evidence of the locked doors and the frilly decor of her bedroom seemed to support my original conjecture: that we had in fact lived separate lives. If so, our reconciliation must be ascribed to the accident, to the sharing of terror and grief climaxed by her compassion for all I had been through.

In rebuttal, the idea of Judith being motivated by compassion seemed contrary to her character; she seemed much too self-centered to be concerned with such an emotion. (I recalled the long periods she spent at the vanity table, her indifference to the outside world, signified by a refusal to read a newspaper—"Why should I get depressed?") Besides, compassion seemed a totally inadequate word to explain her tempestuous sexual need, which had continued unabated throughout our month at San

Clemente. Judith had been insatiable, like a pent-up bride exultantly shucking off all inhibitions in her surrender to postponed pleasure. Considering this, it seemed unlikely that she could have long denied me the intimacy of her bed. But perhaps it had been I who had done the denying. In that case, could Judith have been guilty of some unforgiven act? What? A shameful answer nudged at my mind but I instantly dismissed it. I resolved simply to ask Judith about the room. I would do it the next day, when we were relaxed over cocktails.

Now, pacing in a circle around the fallen oak, eyes surveying the ground, I felt a stab of contrition. Simply because of a locked room, for which there was doubtless an innocent explanation, I had imputed to Judith vanity, callousness, selfishness. All this for a wife who had demonstrated her devotion throughout a harrowing period of horror and pain, who had restored my self-confidence by lavish displays of affection. More practically, a wife who had thoughtfully secluded me at the beach house, thus providing the therapy that had accelerated recovery.

I rubbed a hand over my face with some satisfaction. The skin was smooth and tight, deeply tanned, the scars all but invisible. There was still a numbness in the left cheek where the nerve ends had been damaged but otherwise my face felt normal. My body had been made lithe and tough by vigorous swimming in the sea. Physically, I was once more a whole man. And for that I owed a great deal to Judith.

What feeling was there besides gratitude? Often I had asked myself that question. Passion, yes. But passion alone, no matter how frequently expressed, lacked the vitality of love. Did I love Judith? I winced. I did not know. In my blank world, love seemed as much a stranger as the woman herself. I felt no deep need of her. She was simply an attractive woman with whom I enjoyed sleeping and to whom I owed an obligation. I felt like an ingrate, but there it was.

Rationalizing, I told myself that not until the return of memory, releasing me from frustrating self-absorption, could I be expected to have the capacity for selfless love. That my memory would return I never doubted. Perhaps a piece at a time, slowly at first, as with a jigsaw puzzle, and then possibly in a burst of speed as the picture filled in. It was the way Dr. Stryker and Dr. Ragensburg had suggested it might happen. Dr. Ragensburg had written down the name of a psychiatrist in San Francisco who might be of help. I had tucked it in my wallet, hoping never to need it. Optimistically, I thought that a return to familiar scenes and habits would act as a catalyst uniting past and present. But I had not waited for this as a solution. From the moment of regained consciousness and the realization of my condition, I set to work attempting to illuminate my previous life. Alone, staring at the ceiling, I sifted my mind in a desperate search for scraps of the past. Thwarted, I willed myself to relax every muscle and empty my brain, hoping that dreamlike images would float in and there be trapped. But all that ever entered was the kaleidoscopic nightmare of the hurtling car, and even that could have been based on no more than Judith's vivid description.

I played mnemonic games with myself: studying the driver's license in my wallet in the hope that my photograph, physical description and date of birth would strike a reminiscent chord; examining my body for any pre-accident telltale scars (there were none); pursuing the financial pages of the newspaper for some revelatory name or news item; awkwardly writing my name over and over again, vainly seeking identification with my former self.

As I now prowled the ground where memory had been obliterated, I again had the feeling of playing a futile game, this time a charade aimed at re-creating the broken insensible figure that had been myself. I moved to where the driver's door must have been—unhinged and partly open, Judith had said, framing my blood-soaked head, the rest of me tangled in the crumpled seat, the shattered steering mechanism, the shards of glass. Walking away, I went to a spot where Judith might have dragged my body. Crouching down, I reached through the ugly yellow grass and rubbed my palms across the crusted earth. What did I hope to find? Dried blood? A lost possession? Something, anything, that might start a chain reaction of recognition. I found nothing.

I stood up and swung around the rear of the imaginary car, strolling a dozen feet beyond. Suddenly my ankle turned and I dropped almost to one knee, letting out a short cry. I limped away two steps and bent to rub the ankle. It was not serious, the pain quickly faded. Stepping back, I poked a foot searchingly into the grass, striking a hard, round object. I stopped and picked it up. It was the bowl of a pipe, bleached almost white and joined to a curved but jaggedly broken stem.

A shaft of light seemed to pierce the dark interior of my mind. Within its beam smoke billowed and swirled. A picture slammed into my head: an instrument panel glowing in pitch darkness, smoke dancing in the light. I saw the smoke gust across the windshield as the car whirled, heard Judith scream, felt my stomach drop away as the car sailed from the road, seeming to pause in midair before it struck with earth-shaking force.

I gave myself a shake and realized I was holding the pipe bowl in a crushing grip. Relaxing, I slipped it into my pocket. Fear sweated on my back, blotted my throat, but was overwhelmed by an enormous exhilaration. An image had penetrated that I knew with certainty was authentic. Memory. Sliding a hand into my pocket, I rubbed the pipe bowl affectionately.

The sound of my name being called pulled my head up. It was Judith, standing on the road above, the very spot where the car had leaped into space.

4

I came up to her breathing heavily, as much from excitement as from the climb. She stood with arms folded across the bosom of her yellow shift, her expression a mixture of anxiety and displeasure, as if recovering a little boy who had wandered off and become lost.

"Whatever possessed you to go down there?" Irritation seeped through her flat tone.

"I'm not sure. I knew it was where the car cracked up."

She frowned. *"How* did you know?"

"I can't explain it. But somehow I knew last night when we drove past." I smiled. "Subconscious memory, perhaps."

Her face softened slightly. She returned the smile. Forced, I thought. She probably resented being left out.

"Did it help?" she said. "Help you remember anything?"

"Just being there didn't. But I found something that . . ."

I stopped seeing her stiffen. "You . . . found something?" She turned away and gazed down the long, shadowed valley.

"Yes." I slipped the broken pipe from my pocket and held it out. "This."

She stared at it, letting her breath out slowly.

"It brought something back to me," I said. "Not much, but something. I thought of smoke coming from the pipe. Then, all at once, the smoke became vivid. I saw it in the light from the dash as we went off the road."

Her eyes, bisected by vertical lines, still fastened on the pipe.

"Did I smoke a pipe? Is this mine?"

Her face cleared. Almost sighing, she said, "Yes, you smoked a pipe." She paused. "That is, when you weren't smoking cigarettes. You were trying to cut down. And for all I know, that could be your pipe."

I looked at her with anticipation, waiting.

"Oh," she said, making an effort to smile. "That's fine, Dan. About remembering."

As we walked to her white Thunderbird, it occurred to me that her reaction was hardly jubilant. I thought again of the locked room. Did she have reason to fear the return of memory?

I didn't wait for the cocktail hour to ask her about the room. I might have, but Ginnie Scott had called in my absence to invite us for cocktails and dinner.

I groaned. "Must we? Our first night home?"

It was not yet noon and we were stretched out on yellow divans in the shade of the house overhang facing the pool. Judith was painting her toenails, concentrating on them like a watchmaker adjusting a delicate mechanism.

"I know," she said sympathetically. "But Ginnie and Jeb

are so anxious to see you. After all, they're our dearest friends, and he *is* your partner."

The word made me shudder. It reminded me that I was determined to go to the office the following Monday, at least for a few hours. The idea of mingling with my former colleagues, strangers now, was frightening.

As if answering the thought, she said lightly, "It's not as if you haven't been exposed to people. Remember Tijuana? The horse races, the bull fights?"

We had taken a number of trips across the border during the last ten days of our stay at San Clemente. Judith had seemed restless, so I suggested the diversion. Also, it was a way of sneaking back among people protected by anonymity. The memory was pleasant.

"God yes. And I also remember sitting on those damn-fool zebra-striped donkeys while that fat Mexican took our picture."

She laughed. "You chickened out on wearing the sombrero."

"I felt silly enough without one of those things perched on my head. But it was fun." I reached across and touched her shoulder. She finished coloring her toenails, set down the paraphernalia and grasped my hand. She rubbed her palm lingeringly against mine. Now, I thought, now when it will have shock. "I gather fun is something we *didn't* have before the accident."

She released her hand. It clenched into a fist against her thigh.

"What do you mean?" she said in an unnatural voice.

I answered gently, "I mean the locked bedroom next to yours. You seem to have shut me out."

She lit a cigarette and inhaled deeply before replying in a monotone: "I knew we'd have to face up to this. I guess it might as well be now." As she puffed rapidly, staring out at the pool, I remembered her reluctance to return to Kentwood. ("Why not take a year off, Dan? We could travel.")

She said, "It all started years ago. Both of us finally wanted a child. When I at last got pregnant, we were both very happy about it. But I lost the baby in the third month. It was pretty horrible. The doctor didn't fault either of us. It could happen to anybody, he said."

I moved to her side and touched her cheek. "Judith, I'm sorry."

She made a disparaging face. "Oh, it was all so long ago, as though it had happened to someone else. The really bad part of it was the way it affected our marriage. We'd sort of been drifting away from each other for some time, and when I flunked out with the baby, we split wide apart. I think at first you were afraid to make love to me, afraid I'd become pregnant again. I knew *I* was afraid, and I felt so damned—inadequate. You buried yourself in business and I, well, I became the frivolous wife—too many cocktails, too much bridge, too many fashion shows. You started working late, sometimes at the office, sometimes in that locked bedroom. More and more often you slept in there—you didn't want to disturb me, you said."

"You mean we just stopped sleeping together without even talking about it? Without any scenes?"

"Yes, as simple as that. Oh, for awhile, after a party when we'd had a lot to drink, you'd sometimes come to my bed. We'd make routine love, without either of us saying a word. And there'd be no cigarettes afterwards. We wouldn't speak of it the next day."

I shook my head in bewilderment. I couldn't identify with the degrading situation she described.

"Then it stopped entirely. And one day I found your door to the bathroom locked. You used the one across the hall. I didn't feel shocked or even disturbed, really. It all came about so gradually that it began to seem a completely plausible way to live. We still dined together, we still visited friends together and occasionally entertained them, we still communicated after a fashion—small talk, household decisions, that kind of thing. But we didn't share a bed and what goes with it. When I redecorated my bedroom, you hardly seemed aware of it."

"My God, it all sounds awful."

"Not really. It would be awful now, but not then. We'd given up on each other. And we had separate interests, insubstantial as mine were."

"If we'd given up, then why the trip to Mexico? Why that night on the divan in Puerto Vallarta?"

"Ginnie and Jeb insisted we come along. They'd already decided on it for themselves. Jeb said you'd been working too hard, and Ginnie, well, she was almost pathetic the way she wanted someone besides Jeb to play with. Jeb doesn't rate very high on playing, and he's inclined to treat

Ginnie like some idiot child. Poor Ginnie. She was heart-broken when they had to postpone the trip."

"Postpone it? But I thought they were with us."

"Not until later. Jeb had a sudden crisis in the office, something to do with a new stock issue. Anyway, it took him almost two weeks to clear it up. They joined us for our third week—at Puerto Vallarta. They toured Mexico for a short while after we went home. Anyway, we took off for Mexico by ourselves."

I smiled at her, hoping to erase the anguish clouding her eyes. "And there came the great reconciliation."

She shifted uncomfortably on the divan. "I'm afraid you didn't exactly sweep me off my feet. We had twin beds at every hotel and we stayed in them. Separately. But the big wall slowly began to crumble. We danced together and saw the sights together, and laughed and drank together. By the time we got to Puerto Vallarta, you seemed to have forgotten all about business and wanted to stay up most of the night. The same with Ginnie. She and Jeb arrived at the hotel soon after we checked in. You'd think she'd just broken out of prison. Anyway, you and I had begun to remember how we'd once been. Sometimes I'd catch you looking at me in the way you used to, before we were married and right after." She sighed and gave her head a shake, the long black hair flagging out. "But you never came to my bed. And I never came to yours. I'd lie there wanting to—sometimes alone; you'd still be in the bar and I'd think how surprised you'd be if you came up and got into your bed and found me there. But I didn't have the nerve."

"Until—"

"Until that last night." Her mouth wore a tight smile and her eyes glittered. "I couldn't, or wouldn't, wait any longer. We were alone there in the dark beside the pool, under the trees. We'd been drinking champagne. There was a moon and, somewhere, a Mariachi band." She was looking past me into space, finishing with a look of humorous satisfaction: "So, I attacked you."

I attempted a casual tone. "I gather I didn't resist."

Her smile filled out as she brought me into focus. "Darling, you were *most* cooperative. Though, I think, somewhat dismayed."

"And then?"

Her face became grave. "Then we went home. It was almost Christmas. You had a lot of catching up to do at the office and I began to think, well, back to the old routine. You treated me—awkwardly—as if you were embarrassed at what had happened in Puerto Vallarta. But also as if maybe you'd like to try it again. You never got around to it. It suddenly was New Year's. The accident happened."

There was a long pause. Finally I said, "Before that, weren't you afraid of becoming pregnant again?"

"No. By that time there was the Pill." She squeezed my thigh. "But I'm not afraid anymore."

"You mean you'd like to try again for a child?"

"Not just yet. I'd like to wait awhile."

I felt a need to test her. "Until my memory returns? Until you can find out how *that* Dan Marriott feels about you, and you about him?"

She was silent for a moment, frowning. "No, I think I'm sure about us now, no matter what. It's only that I want to stay attractive for you, while it's all new and exciting."

I stood up uneasily. "Of course, we may never have to put ourselves to the test. As Dr. Ragensburg said, my memory may never come back."

Her eyes flashed an odd look as if the thought of a permanent blackout was not unwelcome. But she said, "Nonsense."

I turned toward the pool, feeling strangely forsaken. Unaccountably, I was suddenly wary of accepting the story she had told.

Over my shoulder, I said, "I'm curious to see the room—the locked one."

5

Judith got the key from where she had tucked it beneath the lingerie in her bureau drawer. Handing it over, she said, "I imagine you prefer to be alone. I'll be downstairs." She followed me out and turned left to the stairs, saying banteringly, "Just don't get any ideas about moving back into that room."

Did her voice sound strained? If so, why shouldn't it? It must have been an ordeal to brief me on our former life. Why didn't I find her story entirely convincing? Perhaps a rehearsed quality to her tone, her phrasing. But naturally she had rehearsed it; the necessity eventually to explain must have haunted her ever since she learned of my memory loss. I resolved to be more understanding.

When I unlocked the door and swung it open, I had the impression of entering a hotel room. After being sealed off for almost eight months, it still emitted the faint odor left behind by a maid—a mixture of furniture polish and woodwork wax and window cleaner. I closed the door, leaned back against it, and inspected the large, square, green-carpeted room. Off to the left, centered against the wall stood a three-quarter bed with a shelved headboard packed tight with books. Two easy chairs of dark-red leather faced each other beside broad, yellow-curtained windows. A small desk was fitted into the corner, a straightbacked chair tucked neatly into the slot. The right wall, next to the door opening onto the connecting bathroom, consisted of a long closet with folding slatted doors. I walked over and pulled them open. An array of suits and jackets hung from a pole. It occurred to me that some enlightening article might have been left in one of the pockets. I went through each garment, turning out all the pockets. Nothing. Not so much as a scrap of paper or grain of tobacco. It was apparent that Judith had sent out every piece of clothing to be drycleaned during my absence.

In fact, I thought, turning around, the whole airless room seemed to exude an atmosphere of scrubbed sterility, as if a determined effort had been made to remove any residual trace of human occupancy. Or was there a more logical reason? A thought struck with the involuntary swiftness of a muscular reflex: Had Judith fine-tooth-combed everything in search of something I had possessed?

The idea seemed beneath consideration. Still—I recalled her startled reaction when I announced that I had found something at the accident scene, and also my feeling, only a few minutes ago, that she would welcome it if my memory remained forever lost.

Braced against the desk in the corner, I snorted in self-contempt. I had heard of people like this: in some way handicapped, and because of it, obsessed with paranoiac suspicions. Slashing at the air as if to wipe out the thoughts, my hand struck a large metal cannister on the back corner of the desk. I rubbed my knuckles and stared curiously at it. Grasping a round knob set in the top, I lifted the cover. A faint, aromatic fragrance wafted out, telling me what I had already guessed: a humidor, more than half-filled with pipe tobacco. Breathing in the scent, a name dropped into my mind. Swann. *Swann's Way,* a novel by Marcel Proust. I was reminded of a scene in which someone was sniffing a steaming cup of cambric tea, each inhalation reviving nostalgic remembrances. Would the pipe tobacco similarly revive memories? Ridiculous, of course. But I was already thrusting inside the humidor to lift out a sample. My hand froze there. My fingers were in contact with a piece of crisp paper, sharply cornered.

Slowly I plucked it out. A narrow, brown envelope, the flap sealed. Perhaps it was an advertisement inserted to reassure the buyer that he had made a wise choice.

I snapped on the desk lamp, picked up a letter opener and sliced through the top of the flap. I eased my fingers inside, coasting the tips along a narrow, slippery material. Carefully I drew it out. I started in surprise. Film. Four strips of it. I dealt them slowly out on the desk. Each strip contained three frames, and each frame was a color picture more than an inch square.

I pulled out the desk chair, sat down, and pressed one of the film strips against the white lamp shade. The images appeared clearly defined—I could make out two figures in close proximity—but too small to reveal identities or details. I pushed back the chair and pulled out the middle desk drawer. It was filled with neatly stacked stationery, pencils, paper clips and—so unexpectedly that my jaw dropped—exactly what I was seeking: a magnifying glass, about three inches in diameter.

Again pressing the strip of film to the lamp shade, I peered through the glass, moving it back and forth to focus. The picture sharpened. A woman's head lay on a pillow while a man sat on the edge of the bed facing her, his back to the camera. The woman's face was hidden by the man's shoulder. Both of the figures were naked.

Startled, I moved the glass down to the second picture. The man, back still to the lens, was embracing the woman. Her face was again obscured. My pulse quickened. I lowered the magnifying glass to the third picture. The man's shoulders had dropped lower and he appeared to be kissing the woman's throat. Her face was now in the clear.

There was no mistaking the definite bone structure, the full, parted lips, the long, black hair. It was Judith.

I must have held the glass on her face for more than a minute. It took that long to wonder why I was not stunned or overwhelmed with grief and jealousy. I was aware only of surprise and a vague feeling of loss, sensing that I was now cut off from the most direct human connection with the past. Then I felt a surge of hope, mixed however with sharp distaste. Could the man be I, Dan Marriott? Could we have become so jaded with "normal" sex as to pervert the act by inviting an observer with a camera? Or, almost as aberrant, could we ourselves have introduced the camera (one designed to operate automatically) in order to provide later titillation? I rejected both ideas. If Judith had been an accomplice in the voyeurism, the film would hardly have been cached in such a cloak-and-dagger depository. A locked drawer or strongbox, yes, but surely not buried beneath tobacco in a humidor.

I studied the next two strips. Each picture progressed in ardor, the positions of the lovers becoming more erotically inventive. Except for two pictures where Judith's head appeared buried in her partner's loins, her face, strained with euphoria, was clearly visible. But not the man's. In those two shots depicting fellatio, Judith's partner had been required to face the camera. But he had been cut off at the shoulders. I clenched my teeth and turned to the last film strip, pressing it against the lamp shade.

The first two frames once more showed the man's back. His body entirely covered Judith's. Only her slim, highlighted legs showed, the calves bulging as they wrapped around his buttocks. My hand trembled as I moved the magnifying glass to the last picture. The man was rolling off of her, his body and face half turned to the lens. I squinted my eyes. There was an odd movement inside my head as if a small door had suddenly opened. As quickly, it snapped shut. Something about the bevelled jaw, the planes of the creased forehead, were vaguely familiar. I had seen him before—I was as certain of it as I was of the smoke swirling in the dash light. But I could neither name the man or place him. He was definitely not me.

I snapped off the lamp and returned the films to the

envelope. Slapping it against my palm, I moved to one of the leather chairs and sat down heavily, gazing sightlessly out of the window. I could come to only one conclusion: I had to have been the one who hid the films in the humidor, thus, of course, knowing of my wife's infidelity. Had I planted the camera myself, or arranged for someone else to do it? A private detective? That seemed to be the logical answer; I doubted that I had the necessary expertise.

But why had I used my own room, and something as unsafe as a humidor for a place of concealment? Luckily, Judith had not discovered the films. But if I had wanted to make certain of that, I would more likely have locked them away in a bank vault. Perhaps I had been in too much of a hurry to do otherwise.

The fact remained, I had been cuckolded. Questions rioted through my mind. Why did I feel no sense of outrage? Was it because, as Judith had said just minutes ago, I had long since ceased caring about what she did? Because I accepted her adultery as an understandable reaction to my own neglect? What had become of the man? Was he merely a transient lover, one among many, or someone with whom Judith sought an enduring relationship? Had he abandoned her, or she him? Did that explain the frenetic ardor of our reconciliation? When had the liaison occurred?

A hypothetical sequence of events stormed into my mind. I saw myself thrusting the pictures before Judith's eyes. She recoiled, ashen-faced. I demanded a divorce, offering only a pittance in settlement. She raged, whimpered, pleaded, but I was adamant. Stalking off to her room, she brooded, desperately seeking a way out. Perhaps the showdown had come just before the . . .

"Are you going to spend the day there?"

My head whirled around. Judith stood at the door, her mouth curved in a mocking smile. My right hand, hidden beneath the arm of the leather chair, still clutched the brown envelope. Covertly slipping it into my trouser pocket, I stood up, struggling for composure.

"Dan?" Her face was now pinched with concern. "Is something wrong?"

"No. What could be wrong?"

"You look so—I don't know—peculiar. Was it upsetting, coming up here? I mean, did you remember anything unpleasant?"

I was silent, fingering the envelope in my pocket. Then, shaking my head: "No, nothing unpleasant. I guess my look was just disappointment. I didn't remember a damned thing."

She breathed out slowly. Relief?

"Ginnie called. Just wanted to know if she could be of any help. And to make sure we'd be over this evening."

Ginnie. Ginnie and Jeb Scott. Our best friends. Jeb my partner. If anyone had an inkling of what had gone on in the Marriott household, it would be them. Perhaps tonight there would an opportunity.

Judith's arms were around my neck, her hand stroking my hair. She pushed her hips close.

"I said we'd be there." She slid her hand down and unfastened the rope button of my sports shirt. "Meanwhile, we've got all the rest of this wonderful day. Just the two of us."

I pushed up my hand to rub my throat, breaking us apart. "Yes," I said. "And the first thing I want is a swim. It's hot."

Her eyes reflected the sting of the rejection. "Fine," she said coolly. She turned on her heel and flounced out of the room.

6

The new pipe, a straight-stemmed Dunhill of fine shell briar, bit at my tongue as I puffed on it and listened to Jeb Scott, who was sitting opposite me in a handsome Queen Anne chair. The pipe and a tin of tobacco (the same mixture found in the humidor) was a gift from Ginnie Scott, presented in a charmingly shy manner during cocktails. Judith had told her on the phone about my finding the broken pipe.

Jeb and I were alone in the richly furnished library, propelled there—despite Judith's protests—by Jeb's insistence that he brief me on the current status of the brokerage firm. I welcomed the break, seeing it as an opportunity to draw Jeb out on the subject clamoring in my mind. When we first met at the front door, Jeb shook my hand with forced heartiness, his manner studiously casual, as if he had determined to ignore my affliction. In contrast, Ginnie radiated a natural enthusiasm, admiring my deep tan and trim figure, even expressing pleasure at the husky timbre of my voice. A scowl from Jeb silenced her and, after that, during cocktails and dinner, the conversation consisted largely of small talk. No mention was made of the accident or its aftermath.

Jeb inhaled his brandy, sipped it, and set the glass down on the leather-topped table between us.

"I tell you, Dan, it's gotten worse in just the short time you've been away. Gunslingers. The Street's overrun with them. No concern with values, only glamor. Speculation's getting completely out of hand. Unless something's done, it will be 1929 all over again. I was only a boy but I remember. My father was ruined."

There was an echo of familiarity to the words, but the face and demeanor of the man meant nothing to me. Except, possibly, as a type: the confident tilt of the sleekly-combed head, the hint of smugness in the thin mouth under the arched nose and clipped black mustache. It was the imperious face of one who never seemed to have experienced self-doubt. The man now appeared older than the one who had visited me at the clinic. But then, of course, I had been too self-absorbed to really notice. Forty-eight, Judith had told me when we were driving over. Ten years older than I. I had been thirty when Jeb, sole owner of his own firm, had elevated me to partner and expanded the firm to Scott & Marriott.

For several minutes Jeb continued to inveigh against the so-called gunslinger speculators, viewing them as a threat to his own conservative policies. Then he abruptly broke off and, lighting a cigar, eyed me thoughtfully.

"So you think you're ready to come back, Dan?"

I tapped out the pipe in the large copper ash tray and laid it down. "Frankly, no. That is, I don't think I'm ready to be of much help to you. I'm afraid I have no idea when that time will come."

Jeb looked at me sharply. "Still no inkling of the past?"

"No, it's all blocked off. Oh, I feel a certain recognition when I read the financial pages. I seem to remember the car sailing off the road and the crashing, and there are a few other things. But no, it's as though life started when I came to some time in January, eight months ago. I'm hoping that getting back to the office, doing the things I used to, will bring everything back." I took a sip of brandy and said with deliberate emphasis, "Judith has been a great help."

Jeb seemed to pick his words carefully. "I'm glad you're both"—he paused and finished lamely—"together."

I leaned forward. "Does that seem strange, us being together?"

Jeb's eyes glazed over. "No, of course not," he said, studying the ash on his cigar. "After all, you've been married a long time."

"But there was something in your voice. As though you knew that Judith and I had pretty much lived separate lives."

Jeb raised his chin, flattening out the incipient jowls, and looked me straight in the eye. "She told you that?"

I countered: "Did *you* know of it?"

Reluctantly: "Yes. You once told me about it."

"And Judith told *me*. Only this morning." I plucked a cigarette from the box on the table, lit it with a silver table lighter, and inhaled deeply. "Does anyone else know?"

"Not unless you told them." Jeb paused. "Well, Ginnie,

of course. I did mention it to her. But she'd be afraid even to think about it again."

"Jeb, I'd like to know what I told you."

Jeb frowned, shifting uncomfortably. "Really, what does it matter now? You're back together again. That's all that counts."

"It might help me remember something."

He smoothed his mustache, sipped again at his brandy. Placing it on the table, he said bluntly, "All right, Dan. You told me you were thinking of leaving her. Getting a divorce."

A prickling sensation climbed my spine. "*When* did I tell you that?"

Jeb's eyes held steady on mine. "I remember it well. It was at my club. We were imbibing a number of New Year's libations. It was the Thursday after Christmas."

I thought a moment. "And New Year's Eve—when we went to the party here—that was the following Saturday?"

"Yes."

"Did anything odd happen at the party? Between Judith and me? Anything you or Ginnie might have noticed?"

Jeb stood up, he took two steps to the barren fireplace, and rested a hand on the mantel. He seemed preoccupied with his cigar.

"Dan, why dwell on the sad things? If you want to jog your memory, there must be plenty of pleasant areas to concentrate on. Your success. The people who admired and respected you. The . . ."

"What happened between Judith and me that night?"

Jeb drummed his fingers on the mantel. He stopped.

Turning, he said in a low voice, "You had a row. Nothing physically violent. Just words. Hardly anyone noticed. The liquor had been flowing freely for some time."

"Were we still having words when we left?"

"You didn't leave together. Not right away, that is. Judith ran off."

My stomach tightened as though yanked by cords. "Then—how did I happen to be with her when the car . . . ?"

"She came back. She telephoned first to see if you were still here. Then she came back. She'd taken the car. I remember Ginnie pleading with you not to go, to stay overnight here. You and Judith had had a lot to drink. *Everyone* had."

"We left peacefully?"

"As far as I know. On the telephone, Judith said she didn't want to come back inside. She was afraid of another scene. She said she'd park the car down below, next to the driveway entrance, and wait for you. About twenty minutes later, you left to meet her. I walked part way with you and saw you get in the car." Jeb smiled grimly. "When I got back to the party, Ginnie was a bit overwrought. I had to deal with her quite firmly."

"Why did I go home with Judith if I was so damned angry with her?"

Anguish glowed in Jeb's eyes. His voice was self-accusatory. "Because I urged you to. Demanded it, in fact. I was so sure that a good fight between you two—alone—would clear the air. A day hasn't passed that I haven't damned myself for that decision."

I ground out my cigarette. "Where had Judith gone when she left here?"

"I believe she said to a bar someplace."

"Can you remember the name of it?"

"No. I don't know that she mentioned it."

I thought of the hidden film strip. "Wherever it was, did she plan to meet someone there?"

"Oh, I'm sure not. She just wanted to get away. But she hadn't intended to leave you stranded. First, she phoned for a taxi. But they were all out on calls."

"A taxi? You *know* she called a taxi?"

"Well . . ." Jeb hesitated, pulling at his fleshy chin. "I recall she was using the phone in the butler's pantry. I happened to walk in on her. Startled her a bit, I think. She whirled around, then said something into the phone. She hung up and told me about the taxi. I offered to drive her home but she said no and rushed out to her car. Worried me."

"She could have been calling a man."

Jeb's face creased in mild exasperation. "Yes, I suppose she could have."

"If so, would you have any idea who the man might be?"

Jeb dropped his eyes in a bemused expression. "No, I wouldn't." His face cleared. "I keep forgetting your memory's gone. Look, Dan, you were hardly the attentive husband. In fact, you seemed to act as if Judith didn't really exist. She had to react to that, you know. Only natural that she might indulge in some mild flirtations."

"Anyone in particular?"

"No, no, no. All of it quite harmless, I'm sure. Sometimes at a club dance, or at a cocktail party—men we all know and trust. Then, of course, there was that chap in Mexico. Nothing to any of it. Just Judith bolstering her ego. I doubt you even noticed."

"The one in Mexico. Who was he?"

"Let's see. Standish. Ridge Standish. Came to Puerto Vallarta the same time you did. In fact, he struck up a conversation with Ginnie and me at the bar right after we checked in. Turned out he'd met you and Judith in Acapulco. Interesting fellow, as I recall. Believe he'd been touring the country."

"And you say—Judith was interested in him?"

Jeb shook his head impatiently. "Dan, stop trying to make something out of nothing."

Nothing? When I had seen conclusive evidence of my wife's unfaithfulness? I set my jaw, persisting:

"Jeb, did I tell you *why* I wanted to divorce Judith?"

Jeb re-lit his cigar, taking a long time. "Nothing specific. You'd grown apart. You weren't getting along. You were both young enough for another chance." Jeb chopped at the air. "Now that's changed. The accident had one good result, thank goodness—it saved your marriage." He stood up. "Now, Dan, I'm asking you, for your own good, to quit this line of thinking. Forget it!"

I heard the heavy door behind me open. I turned. It was Judith.

Smiling, though her voice was edged with annoyance, she said, "I hate to break up this stag smoker. *But.*"

Looking relieved, Jeb waved his cigar at me. "Shall we join the ladies?"

As we entered the living room, the Oriental houseboy was just leaving, having set a tray of assorted liquors on huge round cocktail tables. The room, unlike the library, was furnished in contemporary style. Ginnie Scott sat on a long, curved, off-white sofa, dropping ice cubes into a tall glass. She looked up at me with her demure smile.

"Judith and I are having scotch. Would you like . . ."

"Brandy," Jeb said curtly. He looked at me and I nodded.

Obeying a fluttering gesture from Ginnie, I slid in next to her, while Judith and Jeb faced us at an angle on the sofa. Observing Ginnie as she poured the drinks, I noted again, as I had during her tearful visit to the clinic, the timidity that seemed to characterize her every action. When Jeb ordered brandy—*ordered* was the only accurate word—her hand had jerked nervously to the brandy decanter. Earlier, during cocktails and dinner, she had constantly subordinated herself to her husband, her conversation consisting only of transitional phrases designed to cue him gracefully to what obviously were his favorite subjects. When Judith had sought to discourage our retreat to the library, apprehension glimmered in Ginnie's eyes. Even when presenting the pipe, she had cast anxious glances at Jeb, like a small child fearful of monopolizing an adult guest. The total impression was one of a woman scared to death of incurring her husband's displeasure.

Her grooming and manner of dress accentuated the impression. Her gown, of some loosely-cut gray material, offered only the merest suggestion that she was a woman possessed of breasts and hips. Except for a plain gold wedding band, she was naked of jewelry. Her brown hair, bobbed modestly, framed an oval, rather pretty face with large, unembellished eyes, a pleasantly wide, unpainted mouth, and a dimpled chin. She appeared colorless, but close examination disclosed a potential for beauty. When Jeb had married her she was only eighteen, eleven years younger than he, and the sole child of a rigidly moral widower. Had she married, I wondered, in order to escape a domineering father, only to acquire an equally domineering husband? Had the same desire to flee paternal authority driven their daughter Mary, also a lone child, to insist on attending an eastern college, Wellesley, and to spend the summer with her roommate in Connecticut? These had been Judith's suppositions, expressed offhandedly when we were dressing for the evening. They seemed valid.

I was snapped back to the conversation by Jeb's voice, steely with rebuke: "Of course he doesn't remember, Ginnie! Don't you ever *think?*"

I looked at Ginnie. Her face was flushed and she was biting her lip.

"Sorry," I said. "My mind was wandering. Remember what?"

Head bent dejectedly, Ginnie said, "Nothing—nothing really. I *wasn't* thinking."

"Ginnie was talking," said Judith evenly, "about one night in Puerto Vallarta. We'd gone bar hopping in that pitch-black town and forgot where we parked the car. Some Mariachis loaded us into their Jeep and drove us back to the hotel. Much wild singing."

I glanced sympathetically at Ginnie. "It sounds worth remembering," I said gently. "And I'm glad you brought it up."

Ginnie shot me a grateful look.

I turned to Jeb. "Jeb, you and Ginnie are my closest friends. I don't intend to lean on you, but I'll appreciate it if you talk about the past as if nothing had happened to me. I'll try not to question everything you say. But sometimes—sometimes I hear or see something that suddenly seems vaguely familiar. Maybe if enough of these things happen, the shade will start to go up."

Jeb stirred uneasily, fingering his mustache, perhaps thinking of our previous conversation. He gazed at me as if I were something unreal, consort of elves and poltergeists, inimical to Jeb's accustomed world of quote boards, charts, quarterly reports. I had the impression that if Jeb had not visited the clinic and glimpsed the post-accident trauma, he might have suspected me of malingering.

"Just as you say, Dan," he said with a starched smile. "We want to help you in any way we can."

But the conversation, even though lubricated by a few more drinks, was consciously manufactured. Judith, appearing tense and watchful, finally excused herself to go to the powder room. No sooner was she gone than the houseboy appeared to announce a telephone call for Mr. Scott. Jeb sprang eagerly to his feet and left to take it in the library.

Quickly, as if not to waste an instant of her freedom from Jeb's presence, Ginnie said, "Did you learn anything important in the library?"

I looked at her in surprise. Her hushed tone, the way she gripped her glass, gave the question a conspiratorial quality. She seemed to want to tell me something if only I would supply the password.

Cautiously I said, "You mean about Judith?"

She nodded. Her eyes were wide with anticipation.

"Judith had already told me we weren't getting along."

I waited for soothing words but she said nothing. Whose side was she on, if any?

I added: "But she *didn't* tell me I was about to divorce her. Jeb *did*."

Ginnie swirled the ice in her glass. Her tongue ran over tightened lips. "Did he tell you why?"

"Only generally. It seemed we'd outgrown each other. Judith was batting her eyes at other men. Perfectly harmless, Jeb said. There was really no one else."

Unexpectedly, Ginnie gave a short, harsh laugh. "Do you believe that?"

The change in her astonished me. No longer was she the meek, colorless Ginnie. Indignation had replaced timidity. I guessed she either knew or suspected Judith's adultery, reacting to it with puritanical outrage. Over-reacting. Shouldn't she be a bit more tolerant of a friend's peccadillos, particularly a friend of the same sex?

I said flatly, "No, I don't believe it. I believe there was another man. Or men."

Ginnie gulped her drink. "Man," she said across the rim of her glass. "*One* man."

I felt my scalp tingle. "Did I know him?"

Ginnie stared into my eyes with hypnotic intensity, as if willing me to remember. "Yes, Dan, you knew him. You met him in Acapulco. His name is Ridge Standish. I don't know where he is now, but I know he was here in Kentwood a few days before the accident."

I grasped her arm. "How do you know that?"

She hesitated. "Because I . . . saw them together. At The Hacienda. It's on the highway north of here. I saw them at the bar, and left before they could turn around."

"Did Jeb see them?"

"No."

"Did you tell Jeb?"

"No."

So perhaps Jeb was telling the truth when he said he didn't know exactly why I planned to divorce Judith.

Deep puzzlement slowed my words: "Ginnie, why are you telling me this?"

She shook her head as if not wanting to answer, then forced out: "Dan, haven't you ever wondered why Judith escaped from the accident with such minor injuries while you were all but killed?"

"She was thrown out, just below the road."

"*Thrown* out? Or did she jump?"

"Thrown or jumped—what difference does it make?"

"She might have *arranged* to jump."

"Are you saying . . ."

I was startled to see her suddenly smile. Then I realized the reason as she looked past me and said in her soft, girlish tone, "Judith, we've been having the *nicest* conversation."

In a daze I listened to Judith and Ginnie plan an all-women theater party for the coming week. Their voices held the warmth of two affectionate and trusting friends. Looking at Judith, I wondered if she was being as hypocritical as Ginnie.

Slowly my mind added it all up: the separate rooms, the adultery, my declared intention to divorce her, the fight at the party—and now Ginnie's damning insinuations.

I could no longer suppress the thought that had been snapping at my mind: Had the accident *really* been an accident? Or, on the morning of last January first, had Judith tried to kill me?

7

The Hacienda was about fifteen miles north of Kentwood, set well back from Highway 101 behind a grove of
tall pines. I sped past in the Porsche before seeing the sign,
painted in broad red strokes on black iron, and had to
make a U-turn to enter the crescent-shaped driveway bor-
dered by huge purple oleanders. The building was a low,
sprawling structure of white-textured stucco interspersed
with strips of burnished wood and topped with a Spanish
tile roof. The large parking area was surprisingly full for
three o'clock on a hot Sunday afternoon.

As I squeezed the car into a space in the rear and got
out, the reason for the crowd became clear: from behind
the building rose the sound of splashing, punctuated by
shouts and laughter. So The Hacienda was more than a
restaurant and bar; it was also a rather plush motel.
Made to order for people like Judith and this fellow—
what was his name? Standish, Ridge Standish. They
would meet in the bar, he would stroll to the lobby and
check in, then she would saunter out to the pool, drink
in hand, and simply fade away to the room where he

waited. Dangerous, perhaps, but much more convenient, and somehow safer, then going to a large San Francisco hotel.

It had taken patience, and the help of fatigue, to get away from Judith. We had got up rather early, slightly hung over, and lazed about the pool reading the Sunday papers. Shortly after two, she yielded reluctantly to her yawning drowsiness and went upstairs to nap. Ten minutes later, peeking in, I saw she was dead asleep. I immediately took off.

I had no idea what I hoped to learn by visiting The Hacienda. It seemed pointless merely to seek confirmation of Ginnie's assertion that Judith had been involved with another man. I already had that evidence on the film strip. And it was nonsense to think that my visit could provide an answer to my own silent query: Had Judith tried to kill me?

Thinking of that question later, it struck me as a preposterous notion. Granted Judith and I had been estranged. Granted even that my neglect may have made her consider going off with another man. But kill me? Fantastic. Yet I was needled by doubts. I recalled Jeb's report of Ginnie's distress when Judith had returned for me after running out on the New Year's Eve party: ". . . Ginnie pleading with you not to go" . . . "Ginnie was a bit overwrought." Could she have had specific foreknowledge of disaster? Had Judith herself, drunk perhaps, recklessly confided to Ginnie a desire to do away with me? Had Ginnie at first discounted the threat, then believed it fulfilled by what others accepted as an accident? Or was Ginnie seeking to avenge some personal grievance against Judith? Was she jealous of Judith's aggressive attractiveness, possibly outspokenly admired by Jeb? I wondered if Ginnie was emotionally disturbed. Her suspicions could be symptomatic of at least a mild paranoia.

And what about *now*? Would a woman who had detested me enough to attempt to take my life now be so ardently eager for my company?

There remained the one circumstance which might have made Judith consider murder: if I had shown her the pictures taken from the film strip and demanded a divorce that would impoverish her. That possibility I could not dismiss.

I had gone through the lobby and turned right into the softly-lit bar. It was occupied only by a young man in a red sports shirt drinking beer, a green-jacketed bartender, and a man sitting against the wall thumbing through receipts. Only the bartender looked at me. I slid onto a stool far from the beer drinker and ordered a scotch. The bartender, fat-faced, mustached and crowned with black, springy hair, poured the drink and observed that the weather was hot.

I agreed, picked up the glass and waved it toward the pool area. "Looks like it's good for business."

He screwed up his face and gave a Latin shrug. "For the rooms, yeah. Not so good in here. The swimmers, they bring their own."

I threw a five on the bar. "I imagine you get a lot of regulars."

"Yeah." He turned to the gleaming cash register, rang up the sale and returned my change with a receipt. He glanced at the man working under a small bright lamp against the wall. He was heavy set, his broad face gray in the reflected light, his hair cut to a stubble. "We got a good place here," the bartender said.

The stubble-haired man against the wall looked up, started to smile, then as I looked at him expressionlessly, bowed his head quickly over his receipts.

I reached into the side pocket of my light sports coat and drew out the picture of Judith that I had slipped from its frame. It was the same one I had had at the clinic; earlier, I had taken it from my bureau drawer where Judith put it when she unpacked. She would have no reason to look for it.

I spoke to the bartender in a low voice: "I'm looking for a woman who used to come in here quite often. You probably don't know her name, but here's her picture."

Polishing a glass, he stepped forward and craned his neck over the picture lying flat on the bar. His protuberant eyes rolled up to meet mine. "You a cop?"

"No. Just an old friend. I've been away for some time." I could feel the man against the wall eyeing me.

"Don't know her," the bartender said. A stool scraped the floor and he darted a glance to his left. "But I been here only a few months."

Disappointed, I picked up the picture. A hand touched my elbow.

"Excuse me, please. Aren't you Mr. Marriott?"

I started, spun half around, and looked into the pale meaty face of the man who had been sitting against the wall. He offered a tentative smile showing white, even teeth that obviously had been bought.

"Why . . . yes." I thought quickly. It might be helpful to pretend I knew him. I smiled. "You're . . ."

His smile widened to a toothy grin and he stuck out his hand. "Costa. Ralph Costa. The manager. A long time since you come in here."

I raised my arm stiffly and shook his hand, unable to speak. It had never occurred to me that I might have been a familiar customer.

Costa's face sobered. "Sure," he said, as if to himself. "That crazy accident. It was all in the papers. Damn near killed you, I read." He patted his stiff brush of hair. "You look okay now. Thinner. That's why I wasn't sure it was you."

"I'm fine," I said and took a gulp of the scotch. Turning back, I suddenly went rigid. Costa was staring at the photograph that still lay on the bar.

Thick eyebrows arched, he pivoted his head slowly to face me. "Friend of yours?"

I hesitated, thinking of an answer that could go either way. Forcing a smile, I said, "Well, not a friend exactly." Seeing his face go blank, I added as if half joking, "You don't know her?"

"Sure. Sure, I know her. For awhile she used to come in here about every day. Maybe eight, nine months ago.

Afternoons. Every afternoon. Then all of a sudden we never see her again. I figured she moved out of the county."

It was clear he was unaware she was my wife. Casually I picked up the photograph and slipped it into my pocket.

"Yes," I said conversationally. "I knew she used to come in here. I thought perhaps you or"—I glanced at the bartender who had moved down the bar—"someone would know where she could be found. I lost track of her when I was in the hospital."

"Hmmm." Costa tapped pudgy fingers on the bar. "Maybe she married that guy she was always meeting here. You know him?"

I caught my breath. "I don't know. She went out with a number of men."

"Not when she was comin' here she didn't. Always the same guy. Tall, good lookin'. Let's see." He gave me a measuring look. "Maybe I could find out."

"I'd appreciate that."

Costa waved to the bartender. "Buy Mr. Marriott a drink." He turned on his heel and marched out the door to the lobby.

He was back before I had half finished the second scotch. He brought his mouth close to my ear and said, "Stanton. Richard Stanton. No address. Just San Francisco."

Richard Stanton—Ridge Standish. Close, and the same initials.

"Course," Costa said, "that don't mean that's his real name. But it's the name he wrote down."

I tried for a tolerant smile. "I gather they used more than the bar facilities."

Costa grinned. "That I don't never talk about."

I raised my glass. "Thank you. And thanks for the information."

Costa flashed his teeth, nodded and turned as if to go. He stopped. "Oh. Wasn't your wife with you in that accident? How is she?"

The drink lumped in my throat. "She's fine. She wasn't hurt seriously."

"A nice woman," he said. "A real lady."

For a moment the full significance of the remark did not penetrate. Then my heart gave a big thump. Who was the man talking about?

Cautiously I said, "She'll be surprised you remember her. Pleasantly surprised."

Costa chuckled. "In my business, I *remember*. And your wife I remember very good. Yes, a real little lady. You bring her in again soon."

I was too stunned to pursue it. It was all I could do to down my drink and affect a nonchalant exit.

The irony of the situation swept over me as I pushed the Porsche to eighty down the highway. Here I had self-righteously been damning my wife for cuckolding me and I apparently had been guilty of the same offense. Had Judith known about it? Had her own behavior been simply retaliatory? No, I thought, to both questions. If she had known there was another woman, she would have been able to secure unchallengeable grounds for a divorce and a substantial settlement. Surely she would not have hesitated to establish evidence of my infidelity if she and this other man, Standish, were in love. Moreover, she would have had an overwhelming incentive to entrap me if I had shown her the pictures taken from the film strip (although she might not have had time to act before the alleged accident occurred).

I was seething with curiosity about the identity of the girl Costa assumed to be my wife. (My God, had I introduced her as Mrs. Marriott?) Someone from the office? That seemed most likely. I felt a sickening apprehension. Tomorrow I would be returning to work. Would I also be returning to a mistress?

When I got home I went upstairs and quietly entered our room. I had been gone just over an hour. Judith was still sleeping, lying on her side, hands tucked childlike under her chin. I stood for a minute looking at her face, angelic in repose. It was difficult to associate that face with unprovoked adultery, let alone with violence.

Considering my own apparent transgression and the loyal intimacy Judith and I now enjoyed, why was I still so determined to rake up the bitterness of the past? Wounded masculine pride? Pure vengefulness? The answer came with slow positiveness. Every witness—Jeb with his charitably qualified remarks, Ginnie with her direct accusation, Costa with his unknowing revelation, even the ogling camera with its graphic honesty—seemed to agree that Judith's affair with Standish had flourished just before the accident.

Attempted murder could not be ruled out. It would be impossible to go on living with Judith without settling it once and for all. Obviously I could not find out by simply putting the question to Judith. There might be one other way—find Ridge Standish.

And then? I didn't know.

8

The view from the twenty-ninth floor of the Wells Fargo Building was spectacular. For the better part of an hour I sat in my corner office gazing across the hills of the magnificent white city, out to the sparkling Bay broken by Alcatraz and Angel Island, to the great red bridge that flung across the Golden Gate and anchored in the county where I lived. On my desk, no more than glanced at, were neat stacks of recent office memoranda, market letters, research reports, file folders of correspondence, photocopies of charts and graphs, all designed to bring me up to date on the activities of Scott & Marriott. Jeb had arranged to have them placed there before I arrived.

Driving the Porsche, I had followed Jeb into the city, parking in a garage that was as unfamiliar as the coveralled attendant who welcomed me with a grin and "Glad to have you back, Mr. Marriott." The block-long walk to the office was just as strange, only the hurrying crowds giving me a hazy illusion of having been there before. Arriving on our floor, the receptionist, an attractive redhead, set the tone for the greetings to come. Her manner was

74

smiling and friendly, but restrained, as if too much effusion might prove harmful. Jeb had informed the staff of my condition, playing it down as "a mild memory loss, nothing permanent." As he escorted me down the thick-carpeted corridor, secretaries looked up, nodding pleasantly, and account executives stepped from their offices to shake my hand self-consciously. I responded with diffident politeness. The uneasy deference accorded Jeb seemed to indicate he was as much a martinet in the office as he appeared to be at home.

The only one who seemed perfectly natural was my secretary, Nancy Mercer. She stood outside my door, trimly attractive in a snug beige dress, hand tossing back long blonde hair in a gesture that was almost a salute. She presented me with a sparkling smile and said lightly, "Hail to the chief. Now I guess I've got to go back to work." She offered her hand as though I were a member of the family. Taking it, I began to feel comfortable for the first time.

After that, I had been left alone with the stacked reports. My first act was to go through the desk drawers. I found only stationery and other office supplies; all I expected inasmuch as Jeb had personally cleaned out my desk and found nothing of personal importance. Next, I flipped open the bronze cover of my desk calendar, hoping to find the top page dated Thursday, December 29 of the previous year, my last day in the office (the same day I had told Jeb that I was considering leaving Judith). But the few remaining pages of the old calendar had been discarded, replaced by this year's, showing today's date in red letters, August 25. I then riffled through the mass of papers on my desk, abandoning them for the scenery outside the huge plate-glass windows in the hope it would ignite a flash of memory. Nothing happened.

Without noticing, I had been nervously thumbing through the pages of the desk calendar. Now I looked down and saw that I had run through the remaining days of the year and was looking at a page headed NUMBERS FREQUENTLY CALLED. The ruled lines below were filled with names and phone numbers and, in some cases, addresses. The handwriting was neat and feminine.

I studied the array of buttons on my intercom, pushed one, and jumped as a buzzer sounded outside the door. Nancy Mercer appeared, notepad in hand. I asked her to sit down.

"Miss Mercer," I said and immediately stopped. She was smiling as if I had said something amusing.

"You always called me Nancy."

"Oh. Well . . ." Again I stopped. Now she looked concerned, as if she might have offended me.

"I'm sorry," she said. "Perhaps I shouldn't have reminded you."

I was disconcerted. "Why not?"

Her white skin flushed. "I shouldn't say things that might make you . . . uncomfortable."

I looked at the desk calendar and back at her. "Nonsense. Nancy, let's get something clear. Whenever I seem to have forgotten something, I want you to tell me about it. Not every little detail. But whatever might seem important. That's the greatest help you can be to me."

Her manner changed to the informal friendliness of our earlier meeting. "Good. I want to help." Her blue eyes, almost violet, flashed mischievously. "I'll start by putting your mind at rest."

"How's that?"

"I call *you* Mr. Marriott."

I laughed but felt a sudden apprehension. Was she implying that I was Mr. Marriott in the office but Dan outside? Costa's words at The Hacienda came back to me: ". . . a real little lady." Nancy Mercer was little and she appeared to be a lady. Could she have been the one . . . ? *Stop it!* my mind said harshly.

I put on a business face. "Nancy, this list of phone numbers—did you write them in?"

She became equally businesslike. "Yes. I took them from your old calendar."

"I wonder if . . ."

"I'll be glad to type up a resume on each name. At least those you're not familiar with."

She had anticipated my request. I thanked her and ran my eyes slowly down the list. Except for Jeb's home phone number, none of the listings was familiar.

"I'll appreciate it if you'll fill me in on all of them. Excepting, of course, Mr. Scott."

"Certainly. I'll have it right after lunch."

"Tomorrow will do. I'll probably leave the office before one o'clock."

"Fine." She rose, picked up the desk calendar, and headed for the door. A step away, she paused and turned back. "By the way, Mr. Marriott, a good deal of mail has come in for you since you left. I threw out the obvious junk. I gave the business letters to Mr. Scott. What's left is in the folder in your personal file."

"Personal file?" I said stupidly.

"Yes. Private correspondence, company insurance policies, that sort of thing."

I felt a surge of interest.

"Soon after you left, Mrs. Marriott was in and went through it. She wanted to be sure your affairs were in order."

My interest abated. "I see. I'll look at it later."

"Also, you left a number of reminders to yourself. I kept them in my desk."

"Reminders?" This time I restrained my interest.

"I guess people you wanted to call. They were written on your desk calendar."

I tensed forward. "I'd like to see those now, please."

Nancy brought me a plain white envelope with my name typed on it. She left as I opened it and drew out a calendar page. The date in red was Dec. 29 of the previous year. Four names and phone numbers were entered on the ruled lines.

I went out to Nancy and retrieved the current desk calendar. Back at my desk, I compared the names on the single old calendar page with the phone listing that Nancy had transferred. Three of them matched up; most likely they were clients. The fourth one read Gus Klein YU 5-0900. Three underscores seemed to give it special significance.

I returned the desk calendar to Nancy, came back and

sat staring at the listing. No memory stirred. Well, why not call it?

I dialed the number. Immediately a lilting female voice answered: "Gus Klein and Associates."

"Excuse me. I'm not sure if I have the right number. What business is . . . ?"

"This is a detective agency. Mr. Klein is the president."

The thought had not entered my mind. I felt my muscles contract. "I see . . . well, thank you. I'll call back later."

I hung up, annoyed with myself for sounding like such an imbecile. For a minute, I just looked at the phone, the implications of Gus Klein's profession seeping through my mind. An idea struck me. Opening a cabinet in my desk, I pulled out the San Francisco telephone directory. I turned back to the Yellow Pages, came to D, and leafed through until I located DETECTIVES. It took only seconds to find Gus Klein. His ad was about four inches deep and stretched across two columns:

GUS KLEIN

and associates

DOMESTIC MATTERS

civil and criminal investigation

DICTAPHONE, SOUND RECORDING AND
PHOTOGRAPHIC EVIDENCE

Strict confidence—shadowing and tracing

24-HOUR SERVICE

There followed a list of subordinate services, official credentials, and a phone number and address on California Street.

The wording of the ad told the story: Gus Klein must have been the man who had shadowed Judith—perhaps Standish, as well—and taken the incriminating pictures. Without thinking further, I picked up the phone and called the number again.

The same voice answered and I asked for Mr. Klein.

"Who is calling, please?"

"Mr. Marriott. Daniel Marriott."

I heard a buzzing sound. A phone rattled as it was picked up and a gravelly voice said, "Gus Klein."

"Mr. Klein, this is Daniel Marriott. You did some work for me last year."

"Marriott?" The voice flattened out, becoming guarded. "Sorry, Mr. Marriott, I can't discuss anything on the phone. Maybe you'd like to come in."

I looked at my watch. Ten-thirty.

"I can be there in about half an hour."

"Good. I'll look for you." He hung up.

Next, I had Nancy bring in my personal file. There was nothing in it from Gus Klein, nor anything else of interest. At ten-thirty I told Nancy I was going out on a personal errand and should be back before noon.

I caught a taxi outside the building and the driver circled the block to California Street, grinding up the steep hill past clanging cable cars. I arrived at Klein's office, near Van Ness, shortly before eleven. The building was an old one, four stories high and built of stone blocks. A creaking elevator took me to the top floor, where I stepped into a venerable lobby furnished with a wooden bench and several ornately carved chairs with seats cushioned in red velvet. I gave my name to an anemic blonde girl slouching at a switchboard in a fumed-oak cubicle. When she said, "Oh yes, Mr. Klein's expecting you," I knew it was the girl who had answered the phone. She announced me, then stood up and pointed to a gate in a slatted railing separating the lobby from a row of three offices. As I swung through, a heavy-set man pushed out of a doorway directly ahead and stuck out his right hand as if it were a pistol.

"Gus Klein," he said in a growling voice. "You've changed some."

I agreed that I had.

Inside his Spartan office, he stood behind a gouged desk, an all-gray man—hair, complexion, suit—and looked at me from a hard face with eyes that seemed to have seen everything in life and remained unimpressed. I guessed him to be in his middle fifties, although he had the tough, square physique of a football lineman.

He waved me to a cracked leather chair and we both sat down. I lit a cigarette.

He looked at me from under tangled gray eyebrows. "You understand why I couldn't talk to you on the phone. For all I'd know, it could be somebody checking up on *you*."

"Yes, I understand." I hesitated before saying, "You do recall my contacting you last year?"

"I do." His finger punched at a manila folder on his desk. "I remembered but I checked the records anyway."

"Do your records show that you arranged for some pictures to be taken?"

He looked slightly puzzled. "That's what it was all about. Your wife and a guy who registered as Richard Stanton. Except the name was a phony."

"How do you know it was phony?"

Gus Klein's eyes narrowed. "Mr. Marriott, you'll excuse me, but I'd like to see some personal identification."

I took out my wallet, flipped it open to my driver's license, showing my picture, and placed it on the desk. Klein stared at it, nodded and handed it back.

"I thought I told you at the time," he said. "We traced the car Stanton was driving. It was a rental. The rental agency had taken his name from his driver's license. It was"—Klein glanced at his records—"Ridge Standish."

Retrieving the wallet, I zipped open a compartment and drew out the brown envelope. I removed the four film strips and handed them to him.

"Are these the pictures?"

He arched an eyebrow at me, took the films, swivelled around and studied them against the light. Swinging back, he dropped them on the desk.

"I'd say they are: We also gave you a set of positives—prints."

I now had no doubt that the prints were either in Judith's possession or, more likely, destroyed.

Klein was regarding me curiously. "What's this all about?"

"Do your records show the date when you turned the film over to me?"

He looked again at the manila folder. "Yes. The morning of December twenty-ninth. I gave you both the negatives and the prints and you paid me off. Cash."

That explained the phone number on the calendar pad—I had apparently called Klein for an appointment. It also explained my bitter remarks to Jeb on the same day, over a wet lunch—that I intended to divorce Judith. Had I also told him the real reason? Was Jeb covering it up in order to protect what now appeared to be a felicitous marriage?

Gus Klein was hunched over his desk, eyeing me with suspicion, as if I had come to get my money back. Grittily he said, "I think you'd better tell me why you're here."

"Mr. Klein, early on the morning of January first—less than three days after you gave me these pictures—my wife and I were in a terrible automobile accident. No other car was involved. My car skidded out of control and hurtled down a mountainside. My wife was thrown out of the car; her injuries were minor. I was very nearly killed. I was in a hospital until a month ago."

Klein's eyes flickered. "Had you shown the pictures to your wife—*before* the accident?"

"Yes. I must have."

"Must have?" his face wondered. "Where are they now?"

"I don't know."

He squinted an eye. "Maybe you'd better tell me all about it."

Briefly I told him about the party at the Scotts, the ugly words between Judith and me, her call for a taxi and, finding none available, her flight in our car and her return later to pick me up, the skid on the road, the crash.

"Who was driving?"

"I was, from the Scotts."

"You're sure?"

"I had to be. When my wife got to me, I was tangled in the driver's seat and the steering mechanism."

"Hmm." His jaw moved forward. "Yet you're wondering if it actually *was* an accident."

The flat statement shook me. "The thought crossed my mind."

Klein rubbed at his gray chin. "You mean your wife *planned* the skid, *planned* to be thrown out just in time to save herself?" He shook his head. "That's a helluva lot to buy."

"The skid could have been accidental. But she might have helped it along. The shoulder of that road is fairly high. If I'd hit the brakes, as I must have, we should have caromed back on the road. It's possible the car was not braked but *accelerated.*" The theory surprised me. Until now, I had not consciously thought of it.

"You mean your wife stepped on the gas?"

I was beginning to feel foolish. Lamely I said, "It's something to consider. As I understand it, she was in a dangerous mood."

"Of course, there's no way of proving it now, one way or the other. Did you talk to the police who investigated, see the accident report?"

"No, but I plan to."

Klein gave me a tough, level look. "Do you want my advice. Right now it's free."

I nodded.

"Forget it. Why try to nail her for something you don't have a Chinaman's chance of proving. You got rid of her. Cheap, I imagine. Settle."

"But I'm not rid of her. We're living together. Oddly enough, quite amicably."

Gus Klein's eyebrows rose ever so slightly. When he spoke, it was with the elaborate patience of a man reasoning with a lunatic. "Now, let me get this straight. You walked into my office, this office, on a Monday, the day after Christmas last year. You said you had reason to believe your wife was playing around. You wanted a divorce and you hired me to get the evidence. A very simple assignment. I took it. I had your wife shadowed and right away we learned she was shacking up with this Ridge Standish at a motel called The Hacienda. We got a camera into the room, inserted it into the wall facing the foot of the bed—a special camera activated by any heavy pressure on the bed. In no time at all, we got the pictures, beautiful pictures, proving that your wife was cheating on you. Those pictures—*these* pictures—were so damning I never even wondered why I wasn't called to testify in court. I figured she took one look at them and knew the ball game was all over, and she gave you a nice, quiet, inexpensive divorce, in Nevada maybe." Klein took a sighing breath. "Now you tell me that this same woman, after cheating on you, tried to kill you. And you end up by announcing that you're still living together. *Amicably.*" He raised his hands slowly, spreading out thick fingers. "Maybe I missed something. Maybe I heard it all wrong."

Now I had to tell him. "No, you heard it correctly. The fact is, I don't remember a damn thing about any of it."

He leaned toward me, then swung half around as I quietly related the aftermath of the accident. The days of unconsciousness. The plastic surgery. Judith's thrice-weekly visits. Most important, the amnesia.

"You mean you've drawn a complete blank?"

"Complete." I thought a moment. "Oh, there have been a few blurred impressions." I cited the violent images produced by the broken pipe as an example. He picked up a pencil and made a note.

I went on to describe the month at the beach house, mentioning Judith's ardor but expurgating the erotic sequences. When I got to the locked bedroom and the discovery of the film strips in the humidor, he murmured wryly, "You didn't exactly choose Fort Knox." I finished by reporting my brief private conversation with Ginnie Scott, her disclosure of the Judith–Ridge Standish affair and her implication that Judith had deliberately contrived the accident.

Gus Klein examined the ceiling. "Now why would Mrs. Scott tell you a thing like that? She have any reason to want to cut down your wife?"

"From everything I've heard, they're the closest of friends."

"Maybe you told her something—before your black-out."

"I don't know." I thought of Ginnie's puritanical father. "I suspect Ginnie's principles are pretty old-fashioned. The Scarlet Letter sort of thing—A for Adultery. That could explain her attitude."

Klein contemplated me for a moment from under hooded eyes.

"I don't see how I can help you, Mr. Marriott. You have the proof, on film, of your wife's—indiscretion. It's still valid. You can use it right now to get a divorce, if that's what you want. As for the suspicions about the accident, without more tangible evidence—and I don't know how we'd find any—I can't do a damned thing about that. If you want to hire us to protect you, all right. But from what you tell me, you and your wife are cozy now and seem to have a good thing going. Why not leave it at that?"

"I can't leave it at that. Not until I know for sure whether or not she tried to kill me. Not until I know why she now appears so devoted. Not until I know if Standish is off in the wings somewhere waiting for something to happen to me." I paused. "If I find out the truth, I may also get my memory back."

Gus Klein seemed to know the answer before he put the question: "And how do you suggest I go about finding out all that?"

"Find Ridge Standish."

He threw a big foot on the desk and pushed his chair to the wall. "I guess that'll do for openers."

"You start with one big problem," I said.

"Which is?"

"I can't pay you anything now. My wife would notice the withdrawal."

For the first time, his grim mouth twisted into a grin, a small one. He glanced once more at the manila folder.

"Looks like I'll just have to consider you a good risk."

I glanced at a huge, old-fashioned safe in the corner. "Speaking of risk," I said, and handed him the film strips.

9

I got back to the office before noon. Nancy Mercer told me that several people had stopped by—all goodwill calls—and handed me a message that Judith had telephoned just after eleven. I was to call back.

I sat at my desk for a minute inventing a story, then dialed. There was a hint of accusation in Judith's voice as she asked where I'd been. She had called only to find out how things were going. I was out buying a couple of suits, I told her, and lied further that I was leaving the office in half an hour for lunch in town and should be home about two-thirty.

I left the office immediately, walked up Sutter Street to a clothing store opposite the garage, and in twenty minutes had selected and been fitted for two suits, which I ordered sent. It was twelve-thirty when I got the Porsche and headed out Montgomery Street toward the Golden Gate Bridge.

I planned to visit two places—the county newspaper and the Sheriff's office. Both were in San Rafael, the county seat, only a few miles from Kentwood. Gus Klein could concentrate on finding Ridge Standish. I would do what I could to investigate Judith and the accident.

Forty minutes later I parked outside the low building that housed the newspaper, put a dime in the meter, and strode inside. A receptionist directed me to the back-issue library, where I was taken in hand by a shirt-sleeved, long-haired teen-ager. Had they published a paper last New Year's Day? I asked. They had. He went to a tier of metal shelves and came back hefting a huge bound volume of newspapers. He slammed it on a bare desk, invited me to sit down, then left me alone.

The issue I was looking for was, of course, the first one in the volume. The story, set in two columns, was on page three.

BROKER NEAR DEATH AFTER
CAR SPINS OFF ROAD

An early morning auto accident following a New Year's Eve party today left Daniel Marriott, a San Francisco stockbroker and Kentwood resident, critically injured and in a coma in the intensive care unit of County Hospital. His wife, Judith, suffered minor injuries.

Mr. Marriott, at the wheel, was driving up the steep approach to his home at 114 Summit Way when a skid flung the car out of control, plunging it 500 feet down the mountainside, where it struck a large oak and was demolished. His wife was thrown out not far below the road. She clambered down to her husband, who was unconscious behind the crushed steering wheel, and dragged him from the wreckage.

After administering first aid, Mrs. Marriott made her way on foot to her home and phoned the police. Two motorcycle policemen of the California Highway Patrol arrived on the accident scene at 4:30 A.M., followed by Sheriff Salvatore Bogano and an ambulance from County Hospital.

The critically injured body of Mr. Marriott was lifted up the . . .

I stopped reading. My eyes darted back a sentence to the words ". . . arrived on the accident scene at 4:30 A.M." According to Jeb, it was about two A.M. when I left the party to meet Judith at the bottom of the driveway. Even in fog, it should not have taken much more than ten minutes to drive to the spot where the car spun off the road. Thus, the accident could not have occurred later than, say, two-fifteen or two-twenty. Two-thirty at the latest. So at least two hours had passed before the police arrived. They must have responded immediately to Judith's call. What had taken her so long to get to the house and phone? It was surely not more than a twenty-minute hike, even allowing for the tortuous climb up the mountainside. Judith must have stayed with me for more than an hour and a half before deciding to go and call the police. Had she remained in the desperate hope someone would drive by and offer help? Unlikely, considering that few cars ever traversed that serpentine road, probably none at that hour, and the fact that, aside from our skid marks, barely discernible in the fog, there would have been no roadside evidence of an accident.

The thought that had been lurking in my mind now pounced forward. Had she stayed by my side, deliberately denying me medical help, waiting for me to die—then, finally overwhelmed by the enormity of the crime, panicked and rushed to call for help? Horrifying as it was, that seemed the most logical answer.

But perhaps the reporter had been misinformed as to the time, or there had been a typographical error. It would be easy to check. I finished reading the rest of the news story, which simply reported minor details, and left to make my second call.

Before I met Sheriff Salvatore Bogano, I knew his face: driving to his office, it stared soberly at me from wall posters and billboards that advised me to REELECT SHERIFF SAL BOGANO—HONEST, EXPERIENCED, DEDICATED.

As he swung through the door on his way back from lunch, he looked only slightly less imposing than the larger-than-life portraits posted by his publicists. Under a bushel of black hair streaked tightly with gray, a huge, jowled face with proportionate features shook with every lumbering step. He must have been six and a half feet tall, with a bulging physique that strained against his khaki uniform and overflowed his leather gun belt.

I got up from a straightbacked chair and introduced myself. Without expression or reply, he waved his white Texas-size hat in a signal to follow him. We ended up at the end of a corridor in a curtainless office furnished in early Salvation Army, the bleakness relieved only by one wall completely covered with inscribed photographs and framed letters and certificates.

"So?" was all he said, but in a soft, pleasant tone, as he thudded down into a swivel chair.

I sat down on a flaking metal chair, repeated my name, told him my address, and briefly described the accident on the morning of January first. Did he remember it?

His big black eyes seemed to become more liquid. "I remember," he said solemnly. "I thought you were a goner."

I thanked him for the help he had given and said, "Sheriff, would it be possible for me to see the official accident report?"

Bogano eyed me for a moment. "Your insurance company would have a copy of the report, Mr. Marriott. Also the Highway Patrol. Why did you come to me?"

"Because I just read the news story that ran at the time in the local paper. You were the only officer whose name was mentioned."

"You mean you hadn't seen the story before this?"

Why was he putting me off? "No. I wasn't able to until now. I was in a coma after the accident. When I came out of it, I was transferred to a clinic outside of Santa Barbara. I got home only the other night."

"Santa Barbara," Bogano said musingly. "Now that's quite a distance. Any special reason why you weren't hospitalized up here?"

Patiently I explained the need for plastic surgery and Judith's desire to get the best specialist available. Bogano's only response was a sympathetic shake of his giant head. Obviously he was not inclined to volunteer anything. Perhaps if I could jolt him . . .

"Sheriff, ever since that accident my memory has been gone. I'm suffering from total amnesia."

He scowled his surprise. He hesitated for a painfully long time before saying, "Then you don't really remember what your, uh, life was like at home before the accident?"

It seemed a superfluous question inasmuch as I had already answered it. But I said, "I only know what my wife has told me."

I was not ready to tell him about the separate rooms, the adultery documented by the pictures, the contemplated divorce. For all I knew, he might do something impulsive and explode the story all over the county. Besides, whatever Judith's transgressions, she deserved a more impartial witness before a representative of the law than I could possibly be. It was enough that I had unburdened myself to Gus Klein.

Breaking the silence, I said, "I thought that seeing the actual report of the accident, getting it first hand, might help my memory."

Unhesitatingly he said, "I'll get it for you." He picked up the phone. "Lily, bring in the accident report on Daniel Marriott. January one, this year." He hung up and said to me, "Ordinarily I wouldn't get the accident report. In this case, I asked for a copy."

We waited in silence until a white-haired, elderly lady in a black dress brought in a file folder and placed it on

Bogano's desk. He flipped it open and scanned it as she creaked out the door.

He handed me copies of a number of official forms, stapled together. The first page was dated January 2, the day following the accident. Skipping through the vital statistics, I came to what I was looking for: "Phone report of accident made by Mrs. Daniel Marriott. Rec'd by officer John McCready, San Rafael Police Hq., 4:28 A.M. Jan. 1. Motorcycle officers Charles Hamilton & Thomas Sugrue arrived on scene at 4:35 A.M."

Allowing for a five-minute differential, the news story was correct.

I rushed through the detailed description of the accident as told to the police by Judith. I saw nothing important that I had not already heard. I handed the papers back to Sheriff Bogano. He glanced through them again and dropped them on the desk. He gazed at me somberly, his great chin tucked into rolls of flesh. I sensed he was interestedly awaiting my reaction.

"I guess it's just as you heard it," he said, watching me.

"Yes." I debated whether to mention the seemingly inordinate time interval between the accident and the call for help. I approached it tentatively: "I thought it had happened a bit earlier."

He sat up straighter, bellying against the desk. "Yes," he said, emphasizing the word as if wanting me to continue.

"You said something before—something about, in this case *asking* for a copy of the report. Was there any particular reason?"

He pulled at the folds of his chin. Then he placed both elbows on the desk and looked at me with sharpened eyes.

"I wondered about it," he said softly. "First, as you yourself mentioned, there was the matter of the time. I talked to the people who gave the party, the Scotts. They both said you and your wife left there, bound for home—only a short drive—about two A.M. The accident wasn't reported until two and a half hours later. Your wife explained that: She told me she was afraid to leave you, that she thought you might die if she wasn't there to help."

Perhaps I could draw him out by playing devil's advocate. "That seems understandable. She was terribly upset."

"Yes, and naturally I accepted the explanation. After she talked to me—she had come back to the accident scene and they were bringing you up—she refused to say another word to anyone. She said she was too unstrung to make sense. And naturally we accepted that, too—the highway police and I." He paused, frowning. It seemed an effort for him to continue. "Then the next afternoon, when the officers finally got to her, she said she'd been knocked unconscious when she was thrown from the car. She said she didn't know how long she was out. It's all there in the report."

My hand had already jerked toward the papers on his desk. I found the part previously overlooked: "Mrs. Marriott said that her fall from the car resulted in unconsciousness for an undetermined period."

"She was distraught right after the accident," I said. "You couldn't expect her to be thinking straight."

"I agree. As I say, I simply wondered about it. It's my duty to wonder. And I did have some reason to. After all, I had put a direct question to her: 'Why did you wait for two hours before calling the police?' It seemed logical that if she'd been knocked out, that would be the first answer she'd give. After I saw the report, I thought I'd better have a copy, just in case any questions came up later." He paused. "Also, there was one other thing." His lips pouted and he heaved his huge shoulders in a disparaging shrug. "Forget it. It's all over the dam. You asked why I got a copy of the report. I guess I'm justifying why I did it, proving I'm thorough. Maybe it's the election coming up. Maybe I'm after your vote."

I said: "Tell me about the 'one other thing.' "

He looked at me shrewdly, making a decision. "All right. There's a high shoulder on that road, right where the car skidded off. It was foggy and wet that night. You'd been a damned fool if you weren't *crawling* along—fifteen miles an hour at the most. I wondered why you weren't able to get the car back under control after striking the shoulder."

Having pretended to be Judith's protector, I felt forced to continue. "You said it for me, Sheriff. I was a damned fool. I'd been drinking fairly heavily. I was probably going a lot faster than I thought."

"I figured." He gave a slight smile. "But I can't arrest you for that now." He looked down at the desk as if trying to shape an amorphous thought into words. When his eyes came up, avoiding mine, he said self-consciously, "Just be careful."

The words, deliberately enunciated, seemed to imply more than a casual admonition. Throughout the conversation, he had given the strong impression that he was convinced Judith was in some way culpable. As convinced, I thought, as I was now. Independently, we had attached suspicion to two facts—the protection afforded by the high shoulder of the road and the time that elapsed before Judith telephoned for help; the latter explained one way to Bogano (she was afraid to leave me) and another way to the highway patrol (she was knocked unconscious).

Would Judith's failure even to inform me of the time discrepancy further arouse Bogano's suspicions?

When I reached home shortly after two, Judith was not in sight. I went quietly up the carpeted stairs, heading for our room and a change of clothes. Approaching the door, I heard small creaking noises indicating Judith was at the vanity table.

I stood outside the door, unobserved, watching her seated profile as she energetically stroked her long black hair with a wide comb. She dropped the comb, pushed her face close to the mirror and inspected the striations under her eyes. Frowning, she stretched her neck, examining her throat for the parallel lines of age. She sighed, dropped her chin in her hand, and let her shoulders slump.

I backed off out of sight, feeling a ripple of pity. I called a warning "Judith?" and walked back to the door. The pity vanished.

She now sat straight and, without any greeting, said icily, "Jeb called. He wanted to be sure you got home safely." Her eyes dilated accusingly. "Where have you been?"

"I decided to have lunch alone and just drive around, get to know where I live."

Her face showed disbelief. Petulantly she said, "After this, Dan, I think you'd better keep me a little better informed of your plans."

I said nothing. I wondered if she now distrusted me as much as I did her. However subtly, I thought, the battle between us was becoming joined.

10

Two days later, Wednesday morning, Gus Klein pushed his square, gray body through the door and crunched down in a chair facing my desk.

"Maybe you should get a license," he said with rasping sarcasm. "That is, if you're set on making detective work your career."

I looked at him, mystified.

"Sheriff Salvatore Bogano. I was in to see him an hour after you." His voice became elaborately mournful. "Please, Mr. Marriott, won't you let *me* handle these things?"

I smiled guiltily. "I *had* to talk to Bogano. Besides, I got some information."

"No more than I got. And you're paying me to get it." He shrugged one shoulder and waved a hand philosophically. "So all right. You and Bogano seem to be on the same wavelength about your wife. Oh, he didn't come right out and put the finger on her, but he sure as hell is asking the same questions you are, and maybe a couple more besides."

"Did you tell him about my wife and Standish?"

"No." Klein plucked a hair from the thicket of an eyebrow. "But I'm sure that Italian Goliath got the message. He doesn't say a thing about you going there. I lead right off by saying I got a sick client with a memory problem and maybe he can get it back if I can get a complete picture of the accident." Klein made a sour face. "That was a great opener. He's catching the same act you gave him, only this time he's getting it from a *detective*. He's *got* to figure that you think your wife has been conning you about the accident. I know Bogano, knew him when I was on the Force. He's ambitious. He's dogged. And he's running for re-election. He'd be just the guy to walk into this case with elephant feet and tip off the whole world, including your wife and Standish." Klein made a smacking noise of resignation. "Well, *then* he tells me you'd been in to see him. He shows me the report, tells me about your wife taking forever to get on the horn to the police, mentions the shoulder on the road—just like you did to me—and then hits me with the two different stories your wife gave out. That was no time to ask him about Standish, but, may God forgive me, I did."

I gripped the leather arms of my chair. "I thought you didn't bring up Standish."

"Not in connection with your wife. I told him he was a friend of *yours*. I said—Jesus, how I lie—that you didn't remember Standish, or anyone else for that matter, but heard he was a great pal of yours and hoped he might help with the memory bit. Bogano sat there like some wop Buddha, but I could almost hear the wheels turning between the ears. I made it all by-the-way, but Bogano's sure as hell bound to put it together—you investigating the accident, him thinking it was a try for a knockover, and figuring you do, too, and now you hiring a private eye to run down a buddy named Standish. I could have cut my tongue out. Anyway, he says he never heard of the guy." Gus Klein took a breath. "Well, let's hope he's got sense enough to dummy up and not break this into a juicy item for the local PTA. Besides, Bogano I don't need. Later I got a line on Standish myself."

My hand, bringing a match to a cigarette, stopped in midair. "You mean you located him?"

"Yes and no. Get comfortable. The story takes some telling."

I finished lighting the cigarette and leaned back.

"Okay, I started where I left off just before New Year's. Remember? Our boy used the name Richard Stanton when he shacked up at The Hacienda, but we got his real name, Ridge Standish, from the car rental agency. At the time, we stopped right there because we had all the evidence we needed—the pictures. Naturally, I wondered where Standish was holed up all the time he was romancing your wife. He wasn't at The Hacienda; I checked that. I started calling the hotels in town and, on the third try, found that a Ridge Standish had been staying at the Mark Hopkins hotel during the period in question. Now the plot begins to get sticky. It seems that this Ridge Standish skipped out of the Mark some time on January first, New Year's Day— apparently not long after the alleged accident. He . . ."

"How do you know it was *after* the accident?"

"Good question. Because a kid from room service brought him up a sandwich and a glass of milk at two-thirty A.M. Standish signed for it. The time and date were stamped on the bill. That was right after you and every-one else—and that includes your wife—figures the acci-dent happened."

"Well, at least he wasn't in on that with Judith."

"An airtight alibi. Anyway, as I say, Standish skipped and hung the hotel for ten days worth of bill, including chits for some fancy groceries. But he did leave a token payment—two suitcases. Markings in the suitcases showed they were bought in a luggage store in New York."

My heart sank. Three thousand miles away.

"New York," I said, as though not comprehending.

"Don't jump the gun. Well, I heaved out the New York phone book and looked up Ridge Standish. There was only one in the book, on East Sixty-third Street. I put in a call just to see if he was there—I wouldn't have told him who I was—and got an intercepting operator who told me the phone had been disconnected. I called the New York phone company's business office and found they'd yanked the phone back in November. Reason? Standish had va-cated the apartment. November, I figure, was when Stan-dish took off for Mexico. The guy in the business office also gave me another tidbit from his records—he told me where Standish worked."

I began to feel optimistic.

"Get this. Standish is a stockbroker. No wonder, down Mexico way, you and your friend Scott welcomed him to the group. Standish works—*worked,* I should say—for a bucket shop named Stone and Whitley, Inc. Actually, a reputable brokerage firm, I learned from my friends on the Pacific Exchange. So I called Stone and Whitley and asked for Standish. That started what I began to think was a psychedelic trip."

Gus Klein hiked himself to his feet, stepped to the window and looked out at the vast panorama of the Bay. "Christ, what a view! Makes my problems not so big."

He came back and dropped into the chair. "The switchboard gal at Stone and Whitley acted as though I was asking for Judge Crater. She got the mumbles and asked who was calling. I ducked that by saying it was confidential business. She switched me to some veepee who, when he heard the name Standish, acted like I was Internal Revenue. Okay, enough of the buildup. Finally, I was talking to Marshall Whitley himself, senior partner and president. Smooth as grease on a china pig. He knew the call was from San Francisco, so he also knew it wasn't just a hello-how-are-you blast. Mr. Standish, says Whitley, is no longer with the firm—can he be of any help? Well, yes, where's Standish now? I ask. Whitley wants to know who's calling. I give him my name but not my occupation. Whitley then asks *me* a lot of questions. Was I a friend of Standish? No, just business. Had I seen him in San Francisco? No. When *had* I last seen him? Well, at that point, I'm beginning to get an aching hunch. Look, I say, I'm a private detective and *I'm* the guy trying to find Standish. Last I heard of him he jumped his bill at the Mark Hopkins hotel in San Francisco. Now if he, Whitley, wants to know any more, he damned well better level with me.

"Then it comes out. Standish and his wife were divorced nine months ago—that was November—and he left late that month on a vacation; the top brass urged him to get away so he could shake out the misery. He hadn't had a real vacation in almost three years, so he planned to be away for about two months. He was due back in the office the end of January. He didn't peep to a soul where he was going, except to say he'd probably roam the country. Well, comes the end of January, Standish is a no-show. You guessed it—our boy Standish wasn't coming back. He'd lit out with more than three hundred thousand dollars in negotiable securities belonging to the firm's customers."

Gus Klein's mouth was stretched tight, his tangled eyebrows raised. "How you like them apples?"

I lit another cigarette from the old one. "Judith sure picked a winner. Just one thing—why was Standish such a damned fool as to retain his own name, in Mexico and here in San Francisco?"

"Number of reasons. It gave him the credentials he needed to move around—driver's license, charge cards, check book. Also, he must have believed he had things fixed so it would take a pretty long time before the embezzlement was discovered. In fact, Whitley tells me, he called the office every now and then to see how things were going. Brassy bastard. My guess is, Standish was keeping his real identity, with all its respectability, so he could cash in the securities a chunk at a time, avoiding suspicion. Meanwhile, he was probably acquiring cards of identification under another name—maybe Richard Stanton. Probably he figured to convert all that fancy paper into green cash before the end of January. Then he could assume the new name and fly far away. To Brazil, maybe, where he'd be safe even if he was uncovered; Brazil has no extradition law. He'd be sitting pretty. Three hundred thousand bucks in his kick—maybe more if he'd saved some of his own dough—and not a goddam red cent to pay in either taxes or alimony."

"Then, enter Judith," I said.

"Right. Standish gets the hots in Mexico and decides to follow her up to San Francisco, were they can play house awhile with a little more freedom. In Mexico, with you around most of the time, he probably didn't get much more than a lick and a promise. Sorry. But you can bet your ass Standish didn't figure to take her away with him. With his big plans, she'd've been poison. As it turned out, your wife got to be poison a lot sooner than Standish expected. Comes the morning of the accident. Now, let me rudely interrupt myself to tell you something, Mr. Marriott. Maybe your wife helped that car fly off the road, as you seem to think. Maybe you were having a rhubarb on the way home from the party and maybe she got strong and somehow pressed her foot, or yours, down on the accelerator. But I think you can be goddam sure it wasn't premeditated. I might believe it was *if* I also believed she was absolutely sure she was teaming up with Standish and that he was broke and they needed your money. *That* only a looney would buy. No, for her Standish just couldn't have been in the cards. He couldn't have gone all through planning that embezzlement, planning it maybe for years, and then taken a chance of blowing everything by running off with somebody else's missus. And he couldn't have been after your money—he had plenty. Besides, he'd just been divorced and it's an odds on bet he'd had a belly-ful of monogamy for awhile. And if you need a final convincer, look what Standish did right after the accident . . ."

"You mean suddenly leaving the hotel?"

"Not just leaving the hotel, but *why* he left. Sometime that day, maybe even from the hospital, your wife had to have called Standish. In my book, she couldn't have gone through that day—you in a coma and expected to go to your reward—without getting the word to loverboy and finding out where she stood. Standish probably gave her buckets of sympathy, maybe even some of that I'll-stand-by crap. Why wouldn't he? He wanted time to put a lot of distance between him and her just in case his name got dragged in. He knew he couldn't stand investigation. So he bolted."

"But why did he leave his suitcases? Why didn't he pay his bill?"

"Very simple. He figured by *not* checking out, the hotel management would take it for granted he was still there. Again, time. That's all he could think of—time to get his ass far away. He had to have taken off immediately after he heard about the accident. What other answer is there? He had everything to lose by hanging around. Christ, how your wife must have hated that tricky bastard after he copped out."

"I guess she had no idea he was mixed up in something crooked or she probably would have turned him in."

"Oh no, she wouldn't do that. She'd have realized that, with the shaky alibi she'd given Bogano—different than the one she later gave the highway police—dragging Standish in would only be asking for a lot more investigation. You'd apparently showed her the pictures I'd had taken, and she knew the films were hidden away someplace. If the cops found them and you died and they knew that Standish had come up from Mexico just to be near her, the investigation might damned well have been for conspiracy to commit murder. If you lived and she kept her trap shut about Standish, she could forget about cops and maybe even throw herself on your mercy, holding on to her meal ticket. No, she knew she could come up winners only by keeping Standish the hell out of it."

It was all brilliantly clear. Abandoned by Standish, fearful of the police, Judith had to have believed that her own security lay in sticking by me. There had been no need to throw herself on my mercy—amnesia had spared her the humiliation. However bitterly, I was forced to admire her virtuoso performance as the ardently devoted wife. Or had it merely begun as a performance and then, uninhibited by our past estrangement escalated to the real thing? Vanity, I thought, the absurd male vanity that protectively insulates sexual pride.

"Naturally," Gus Klein was saying, "Whitley couldn't keep a thing like embezzlement quiet for long, even though the firm made restitution to the owners of the securities. The story hit the New York papers in mid-February. By then, of course, Standish had had plenty of time to switch identities and beat it out of the country, which you can be damned sure he did on or about January one. I don't know how far the law got in tracing him but it's a cinch they got as far as I did. Anyway, as of now, Whitley says they're at a dead end. For all they know, Standish could be lazing around some banana republic playing gin with Martin Bormann."

"Didn't Whitley ask *you* why you were looking for Standish?"

"Yeah. I told him it had to do with some phony checks and unpaid bills. He sounded unconvinced but what could he say?"

"Later, did you tell Bogano about Standish being an embezzler?"

"No. He wouldn't have cared less. He's all local."

I stubbed out my cigarette. "Where do we go from here?"

"Where's to go? If the Feds are stymied, what makes me think I can do any better? You say so and I'll keep at it. But chances are you'd be pouring your dough down a rathole."

I thought a minute. Reluctantly I said, "No, let's call it quits. Send me a bill and I'll get a check to you shortly."

We stood up and shook hands. Gus Klein said, "Mr. Marriott, do you still have a gun?"

"Gun? What gun?"

Klein stepped back, nodding to himself. "Well, sure you wouldn't remember. Anyway, it crossed my mind that maybe, right after you hired me to follow your wife, you might have got yourself a gun. You know, to protect your home, the unwritten law, that kind of crap. So I checked, and found out you *had* gotten a gun permit. But that was a year ago last April, long before you ever met Standish. The reason given was that you'd had a prowler or two around the house. Anyway, I mention it because it might be a good idea to keep that gun where not just anybody can get at it."

I felt a chill. "You mean my *wife?*"

Klein flushed. "Be practical, Mr. Marriott. You figure she tried to knock you off once. Maybe you're right, maybe you're wrong. But why take chances?"

"Funny, my wife never mentioned a gun."

Klein popped his eyes. "Yeah," he said. "Funny."

11

When I got home in mid-afternoon, no one was there. Judith had left a note that she was at the beauty parlor, and the cleaning woman who came in daily had finished up early and left.

I ransacked the house for the gun. Starting in the garage and moving systematically inside the house, I inspected every closet, every shelf, every drawer, cabinet and container. Each time the weapon failed to appear I became irrationally fearful that it had not been mislaid but had been deliberately concealed by Judith, to be used against me when and if necessary.

Gus Klein was not the only outsider who knew I had bought a gun. Jeb knew it, too. We'd had lunch together and I brought up the subject in a roundabout way, hoping I'd be able to quote him as the source of the information when I queried Judith.

Jeb had created the opening with a diatribe against certain city officials, accusing them of being soft on lawbreakers.

At some relevant point, I interrupted: "It worries me

personally, Jeb. Take our house—it's so damned isolated. Judith must have been insane to stay there alone all the time I was away. No protection at all if someone decided to break in."

Jeb rubbed his mustache with a napkin. "Well," he said, "she *did* have your gun."

"Oh?" I said innocently. "I didn't know about that."

Then he told me the same story Gus Klein had, about the prowlers.

"I'll have to ask Judith about it," I said.

And ask her I would, as soon as she stepped inside the house. That occurred shortly before four when I was atop a low ladder feeling along a closet shelf at the end of the upstairs hall.

I stalked downstairs and confronted her in the living room where she was sitting on the sofa going through the mail. She wore a tight, lemon-colored dress and her black hair, perfectly coiffed, was secured by an invisible net. Her greeting was impersonally pleasant as her "Anything new?" routine.

"I had lunch today with Jeb."

She smiled slightly, not really comprehending as she continued shuffling through the mail. "Bills, bills," she said to herself.

"Judith, what's this about our keeping a gun in the house?"

She didn't look up but I saw her fingers squeeze on an envelope, bending it.

Carefully she said, "Where did you hear that?"

"Jeb. I told you I had lunch with him today."

Her face tightened with suspicion. "Now, how would that get into the conversation?"

"We were talking about local crime. Jeb just happened to mention the gun." I felt my scarred voice vibrate impatiently. "All I want to know, Judith, is where is it?"

"I suppose," she said coldly, "you tore the house apart looking for it."

"Just about. Why wouldn't I? After all, you never told me about it."

She adopted an injured air. "No, I didn't. And I didn't because I was simply being thoughtful. Why should I upset you, in your condition, about something that frightened us more than a year ago?"

"You mean the prowlers. Jeb told me."

Her jaw set fiercely. "Jeb seems to be a gold mine of information."

"That's not deserved. The subject just happened to come up." I crossed the room and stood over her. "You still haven't told me where the gun is."

She stacked the letters and held them tightly in her lap. Slowly her eyes looked up to mine. "I got rid of it," she said resentfully. "I've always been terrified of guns. You knew that—*before*. That's why you always kept the gun where I'd never see it—in the desk drawer in your bedroom."

Right below where I had hidden the film, I thought. I said, *"Where* did you get rid of it?"

"My God, what's so important about that damned gun! You'd think somebody was about to get killed with it!" Her face was white. "All right, I . . . I threw it off the bridge." She paused, seeming to think a moment. "I parked the car at Vista Point. I'd wrapped the gun and the bullets in a newspaper. I walked part way across the bridge and just dropped them over." The explanation seemed to relax her. Her eyes softened and she offered a tentative smile. "I was more afraid of having the gun around than of prowlers. Silly, I guess."

And not exactly believable, I thought. But there was nothing to do but accept her story, however hastily invented it seemed.

The phone rang in the hallway by the stairs. Judith jumped up, scattering the mail, and almost ran to it.

"That was Ginnie," she said, coming back and standing at the door. "She can't make the theater party tonight. Not feeling well. I guess it's that time of month for her."

"Theater party?"

"Yes. Oh, Dan, we talked about it the other night at Jeb and Ginnie's. It's a benefit at the Geary. Just a bunch of us women. First, dinner in town and probably a couple of nightcaps after the show. I know, it sounds godawful."

It didn't sound awful to me. At this point, any separation was like receiving a gift. After being home only five days, we already bristled at the sight of each other. I had the feeling she distrusted me almost as much as I did her.

As if reading my mind, she said pointedly, "You don't *mind* being alone, do you?"

"No," I said shortly, "I think it's time we got away from each other once in awhile."

She gave me a probing look and without a word turned and ran up to her bedroom. She spent the rest of the afternoon there, fussing with clothes, emerging just after five in a clinging black dress and exuding a cloud of perfume. The kiss she brushed on my cheek was automatic as she said goodbye and went for her car to pick up three of her friends.

I made a double martini and for awhile, glass in hand, browsed about the house, examining the titles on the book shelves, occasionally riffling through a magazine. Then, in the fading light, I sat out by the shadowed pool, sipping my drink and brooding about where I was going from here.

My position was ridiculous. I was living with a woman who, I was convinced, had tried to kill me, not simply out of drunken wrath but because of her revealed passion for another man. Yet there was neither proof of the intent to kill nor proof that her feeling for the other man was anything more than a passing, though intense, infatuation, instigated by my own aloofness. I could, of course, face Judith now with the evidence of the pictures and demand my freedom. But somehow I felt that after almost eight months of apparent devotion, she had earned parole. And what of my own implied escapade—the girl I had taken to The Hacienda? Was that simply a brief interlude, perhaps incited by jealousy, or had it been a continuing and serious affair, which Judith might even know about and would attempt to use as a counter weapon should I choose to seek a bargain divorce? (*Who* was the girl?)

I thought of going back to Sheriff Bogano and whetting his suspicions with my own in the hope of galvanizing him to root out the truth about the accident. But based on the report and everything I knew, I could only conclude that the truth defied documentation. Further investigation would only stir things up uselessly, perhaps fomenting an intolerable public scandal. No, the whole truth, if it was ever to be revealed, must be sprung from some locked compartment of my mind. I recalled that Dr. Ragensburg had given me the name of a San Francisco psychiatrist. Perhaps that was the only solution. I winced at the thought of resuming those maddeningly frustrating sessions. I would wait a while longer.

It was six-thirty when I came inside. I had looked forward to spending the evening alone, but now I felt anxious and depressed. I considered going to a movie but rejected the idea—I was too keyed up to sit still. I decided to call Jeb. If Ginnie was feeling better, perhaps they would drop over for a drink and we might go out to dinner.

Ginnie answered the phone. She sounded pleased to hear from me, was sure Jeb would be glad to come over, but he wasn't home yet.

"Feeling any better?" I asked.

"Oh, yes, much. I think the idea of being with all those women gave me a headache."

"Good. Well, if Jeb's in the mood . . ."

"Tell you what, why not come over here? We'll have a drink until he gets home. Then we can decide on dinner."

I gratefully accepted, changed into a sport coat, and was there in twenty minutes.

Ginnie met me at the door wearing a white silk dressing

gown, saying apologetically, "I decided to stay informal. Jeb hasn't arrived but we can console ourselves with some nice, cold martinis."

Ginnie poured them, sitting down on the curved sofa. Both of us sat in the same position as when, only a few nights before, she had staggered me with her knowledge of Judith's affair with Ridge Standish. I wanted to reopen the subject but Ginnie's manner, comfortably sociable, deterred me.

She asked whether business affairs had begun to seem familiar.

"Ginnie, it's all one big blank." Then, suggestively: "As you know, I don't have a shred of memory about some really important things."

She gave me an oblique glance but said nothing.

I dropped it. "I'm getting by, but everything is one-dimensional. No reference points, no past associations to round things out and give them meaning. I feel like I've learned everything by rote, that while I may say and do a lot of the right things, I don't really know *why.*"

She watched me intently as I lit a cigarette.

I said, "Maybe what I need is some dramatic experience that will blast away whatever it is that's blocking out the past." I smiled at her over my glass. "I guess that's pretty *melo*dramatic."

"No," she said, drawing out the word. "Perhaps that's exactly what you need." She seemed about to say more but sipped her drink instead.

As we continued to drink and exchange small talk, a subtle change came over her. She became progressively remote, as if preoccupied with apprehensive thoughts. Perhaps, I thought, she went through this metamorphosis every day at this time, adjusting herself to submissiveness before the master arrived. I looked at what was left of the pitcher of martinis—only about an inch, mostly ice water. I picked up the pitcher and stood up.

"I think we need a fresh start," I said.

"Yes," she said, as if speaking to herself. "Yes, a fresh start."

I went to the kitchen, emptied the pitcher into the sink, and got ice cubes from the refrigerator. Gin and vermouth and a partly peeled lemon were on the counter next to the sink. I picked up a small sharp knife to slice fresh strips of lemon.

Suddenly the kitchen was plunged into darkness.

The knife clattered to the counter. For a moment I thought a fuse had blown. Then, turning, I saw in a wedge of pale light admitted by the half-open door, a silhouetted figure standing stiffly erect. I blinked to adjust my eyes. It was Ginnie. Her dressing gown and slippers were heaped on the floor beside her. She was stark naked.

12

My first thought was that her mind had snapped. "Ginnie! What in hell . . . !" She came to me like a sleepwalker and slowly put her hands around my neck. Her mouth was partly open, teeth flashing white in the darkness. Her breasts, firm as small melons, pushed into my chest. I was too stunned to move.

"Dan," she said dreamily. "Dan, it's been such a terribly long time. I couldn't wait another minute."

My body went rigid. Again I said, "For God's sake!" And then, my disbelief becoming total: "Why me? Ginnie, why *me?*"

She pressed her lips hard on mine. I was unable to respond. Drawing back, she said, "Later, Dan, later we'll talk."

"But *Jeb*—he'll be . . ."

"Jeb won't be home for hours. I knew that when you called. And it's the servant's night off."

Vapidly I said, "You and I. Were we . . . ?"

"Lovers, Dan. Wild, wonderful lovers." She kissed me again.

I commanded myself to pull away but could not. I had the sensation of being transfixed by a wraith. But my hands, now involuntarily gripping the narrow waist, told me that this was all substantial woman, warm and vibrant, pores breathing out scent, breath quickening on my throat.

Once more I attempted to protest but the words sank to a faltering murmur. And again she said, "Later, Dan," while her hands stroked down to grasp my phallic hardness.

The vinyl floor was cool and slippery under my hip when, naked from waist to ankles, I lay beside her, resistance disintegrated, consternation postponed. There was the flailing of legs and hips . . . the searching of mouths and loins . . . the straining of flesh and sinew . . . then a whimpering struggle to delay consummation . . . finally an irresistible rushing toward it, arriving in a gasping, dizzying, torrential outburst of energy.

For a moment after completion, reality was only a cold, hard floor pressing against the small of my back. Then it was Ginnie's hand clutching mine and the shocking realization that I was lying on the floor of my best friend's kitchen with his naked and exhausted wife.

I waited a decent interval and said, "We can't stay here."

Ginnie rubbed her cheek against my shoulder, rose stiffly, gathered up her dressing gown and slippers and stepped silently through the door.

When I entered the living room with the pitcher of fresh martinis, she was again sitting in her place on the sofa. Her round face was swollen with residual passion, but her hair was neatly combed and there was a touch of lipstick on her lips. Her hand shook as she took the pitcher from me and poured. Sitting down a few feet away, I accepted a drink, gulped half of it, placed it on the table and lit a cigarette.

I was still too dazed to know what attitude to strike. I tried levity. "I did suggest a dramatic experience. But God. We must both be radioactive."

She smiled remotely into her glass, her eyes bemused. I had the impression she was reliving the explosive episode, wondering about it, perhaps chiding herself on her boldness. Then she gave her head a shake as if to empty it of thought. She drank her martini in one swallow and poured another.

A thought burst into my mind, demanding that I skip the amenities. "Ginnie, did you and I ever go to The Hacienda? By ourselves?"

She sipped the second drink, swallowing hard. She whispered into it, "We went there often."

So at least I now knew the identity of the "real lady" that Costa, the manager, thought was my wife. The knowledge brought no relief.

Suddenly, in a thin, nervous voice, Ginnie began to talk. "We went there at least twice a week. We'd meet about six and stay until about nine-thirty. Judith thought you were working late. Jeb thought I was at a club meeting or off visiting a woman I've known for years who lives in Napa. She knew all about us and would have called me if Jeb should ever phone her. It was never necessary. Sometimes we were together here, but we gave that up as too risky. And sometimes we went to another motel, occasionally in town if you really were delayed. But mostly it was The Hacienda."

I felt a sickening weariness. "How long did it go on?"

"More than a year. Right up until the time of the accident."

Ginnie twisted toward me, gripped my knee and looked plaintively in my face. "Dan, there's no reason for remorse. If ever two people deserved to love each other, it was us. Jeb treated me like a *thing,* a robot that was supposed to run his house, fetch his comforts, attend to his friends, and never speak or show an emotion. As for Judith"—Ginnie's lips curled in contempt—"Judith should have been locked up a long time ago."

I poured another drink. "Why do you say that?"

"For one thing, she's a nymphomaniac. Truly one. Oh, I know that may not be her fault but she could have shown some control, out of respect to you. She was very clever about it. I doubt if anyone besides the men involved even suspected it. Certainly you didn't. *You* thought she was frigid, or at least that sex was no longer important to her."

I certainly hadn't thought her frigid in the past month or so. "How did you know about the . . . nymphomania?"

"She told me. I was her confidante. How it delighted her to shock sweet, proper little Ginnie with tales about her glorious affairs—each one the ultimate. She trusted me because she thought I'd rather die than mention such a subject. And, of course, she had no idea about you and me."

"Judith blamed our estrangement on my indifference, on being married to my job. She said I became that way—that we started to drift apart—right after she'd had a miscarriage."

Ginnie blew out a scornful breath. "Miscarriage! It was an abortion. She doubted you were the father. She was horrified at the idea of becoming a mother. Not because it mightn't have been your child, but because it might spoil her fun."

Beneath my astonishment, anger began to churn. "Did Judith tell you about Ridge Standish?"

"No, oddly enough. But I guessed something was going on between them in Puerto Vallarta."

"And then you saw them together at The Hacienda."

"No, that was a lie. I wasn't ready to tell you the truth. It was *you* who told me he was here. You found out by hiring a detective to shadow her."

"Klein," I said, "Gus Klein."

Her mouth dropped open. "That's right! Dan, are you starting to remember?"

"No. I'll explain about Klein later. But you said I never suspected Judith. Then why would I even think of hiring a detective?"

"Because by then you *did* know. *I* finally told you." She jerked away. "Dan, don't look at me like that. Things had come to a point between us where I *had* to tell you. And you were *glad* I did. Klein got the evidence you wanted in a couple of days, between Christmas and New Year's. Pictures. And he got them at, of all places, The Hacienda. I nearly fainted when you told me that. How did we ever miss running into them?"

I told her about talking to Costa. "Apparently they met earlier than we did and were probably bedded down by the time we got there. He signed in as Richard Stanton. Did I show you the pictures?"

"Yes. They were quite . . . explicit."

Now the key question: "Did I show them to Judith?"

"Oh, yes! You told me there was a terrible scene. Judith didn't deny anything—she couldn't. You told her you wanted a divorce, that you'd give her a small cash settlement but nothing more. She ranted and raved, trying to blame it all on you, saying she was driven to it because you'd ignored her for so long. And I guess you had. You'd even moved into the other bedroom a long time before. But, as you say, that was because you thought she'd grown cold. You didn't mention all her other affairs; that might have dragged me into it. Anyway, Judith finally said she'd have to think about the divorce for a few days. My guess is she wanted to see where she stood with Ridge Standish. That was the Thursday before New Year's. I know she went into town on Friday. Your office was closed and you called me and we met down at the shopping center."

I could imagine Standish's reaction when Judith informed him that he would soon have the privilege of marrying a pauper. Despite his embezzled wealth, much of it probably yet to be converted to cash, it was doubtful if he would want to take on the burden of marrying a woman approaching forty who had nothing substantial to contribute. *Now, if there were some way she could get a big chunk of her husband's money, perhaps even all of it, why then . . .* Is that the thought Standish had planted in Judith's mind?

"Well, you and Judith came to our party anyway, both looking grim. After you'd had a few drinks, I noticed that Judith was getting nasty. Perhaps you were, too, but you seemed in control. I don't know much of what was said, but once—you were standing in the corner over there— Judith came up to you and after a minute I heard her say, 'I'll tell the whole goddamned world you're impotent!' The irony of the year, I thought. Well, that was about it. She called a cab, couldn't get one, and stormed off in her car. She came back about two, picked you up and . . . ugh, why go into the rest."

I thought a minute and said, "You say I was *glad* to hear about Judith's affairs. Why?"

"Because then you knew you could get the evidence you needed for a divorce. I waited until I was sure you wanted that before telling you about Judith." She looked at me wistfully. "Dan, you wanted to marry me."

The answer startled me. Until then I had assumed Ginnie and I were simply playing the suburban sex game. "Did you want to marry *me?*"

Solemnly she said, "More than anything I *ever* wanted."

"Why didn't I just tell Judith about us and let her divorce me without raking up all that muck? Considering her attitude toward me, and her own inclinations, I'd say she'd have been more than glad to."

"Yes, but if you told her about us she'd have squeezed out a lot more alimony. And you and I needed the money. Also, if Jeb knew—and you can be sure Judith would have told him—he'd have smeared me black. *After* your divorce and things simmered down, I was going to tell him about us as though it had just happened. That wouldn't have been quite as damaging to his pride as if he learned we'd been sleeping together for more than a year. I think then he'd have handled it all very quietly. But of course I wouldn't have gotten a cent from him."

"He'd have thrown me out of the firm."

"We expected that. But with your background and ability you could have landed a top position with almost any firm you wanted."

It seemed incredible that Ginnie and I could have maintained the pretense of friendship—she with Judith, I with Jeb—throughout the long period of our clandestine relationship. We must both have been as histrionically talented as Judith.

Briefly I told her about finding the film in the humidor, the phone number on the calendar pad, leading me to Gus Klein, his investigation of Ridge Standish, revealing he had skipped out of his hotel right after the accident and was wanted for embezzlement in New York.

"Well!" she said, eyes rounded. "Now I know why Judith has been playing the loving little wife. At first I thought that perhaps the accident and the terrible time you've had might have accomplished some sort of miracle. But no. She was jilted by her lover and, ever since, she's been hanging on to her husband and his bank account for dear life." A look of grim satisfaction crossed Ginnie's face. "It's certain she got hold of those pictures you showed her and destroyed them. But how that woman must be worrying about where the film strips are!" She looked at me anxiously. "They aren't still in the humidor?"

"No, I left them with Gus Klein. But I think Judith is worried about something else, too."

I had been saving Sheriff Salvatore Bogano until last. Now I reported his suspicions aroused by the time lapse, the switch in Judith's stories, the inference that the car might have been deliberately accelerated to force it over the road's high shoulder.

"As you see," I said, "it's all circumstantial. Not a damned thing can be proved. And it's possible that Judith was completely innocent. None of it might seem exceptionally suspicious if the accident hadn't happened right after I'd shown her the pictures, demanded a divorce, then fought with her at your party."

Ginnie's eyes narrowed, her lips pursed, emphasizing the dimple in her chin. "Does Bogano know about the pictures, all the rest of it?"

"God no. If he did, he might try to be a hero—there's an election coming up, you know—and get us all in the papers. I'm staying away from Bogano."

Ginnie had been thinking. "I remember something now, something you told me when we met in the parking lot the day after your scene with Judith. You said that she shouted at you, 'If you ever dare to use those pictures against me, I'll kill you.' I didn't think much about it then;

just something any furious woman might say. Now I believe she meant it. Do you think Ridge Standish might have been involved in it?"

"I don't know. Not directly anyway." I told her about his alibi—the room service check stamped with the time, two-thirty A.M.

I looked at my watch. Not quite eight-thirty. I poured another drink, deciding to stay only long enough for us to assess our present position.

Ginnie said, "The other night I was watching Judith, wondering if she'd really had a change of heart about you. She kept her eye on you every minute and she was really furious—frightened is probably the right word—when you and Jeb went into the library together. The way she looked made me think: she stands to lose everything if your memory comes back; she hopes it never does. I thought how terribly unfair she was being to you. And to us. Tonight, if you hadn't called here, I'd have called you." For the first time she blushed. "That's why I walked into the kitchen the way I did."

"To shock me into remembering?"

"Partly that." She hugged herself, shivering slightly. "But mostly, Dan, because I've ached to be naked with you every day since you've been gone." Suddenly she slid over and clung to me. "Oh, Dan, Dan, what are we going to do now?"

Disappointment welled through me as I realized I could feel no more genuine love for her than I had for Judith at the beach cottage. Had that former love for Ginnie been born of mutual anguish? Had it been nourished only by sexual response? Was it now dead because I had not even a memory of the anguish and needed no sexual excitement outside of Judith?

Looking up and watching my reaction, Ginnie's eyes began to dilate. She pulled away slightly.

"I think," I said, "that for the time being we'll have to go on as we have. At least until I know what to do about Judith."

My free hand was on her shoulder. I felt her body contract. She stared at me with frowning puzzlement.

I tried offering her at least a token reassurance. "I *will* remember again, Ginnie. Try to understand until then."

She sprang up and backed away, her legs hitting the cocktail table. "I think I *do* understand," she said in a tight voice.

It seemed obvious that she thought I was too dependent on Judith to leave her.

"I think you'd better go," Ginnie said. "Right now."

13

For the next couple of days I was like a man in a pressure cooker. Not only was I tense in the presence of Judith, but also now with Jeb. It was as though he had only to look at me to know that I had possessed his wife, and that he was patiently waiting for me to break down and tell all. I assured myself that his attitude, if it actually existed, was directed only at my general amnesia. Nevertheless, I was conscience-stricken and nervous about every word I uttered.

After having lunch with Jeb on Friday, I got home shortly after two exhausted. Judith was out, as usual, and I could hear Mirabelle, our daily cleaning woman, rattling plates in the kitchen. I walked in and asked when Judith was expected.

Mirabelle brushed a springy rope of hair from her black forehead and looked at me through thick-lensed glasses. "She said two, Mr. Marriott. Past that now."

The phone rang next to the stairs. I sauntered to it and picked it up.

"Hello," I said.

There was no answer. Just the sound of breathing.

"Hello," I said again. "This is Mr. Marriott. Who is this?"

Dead silence. Then I heard a soft click, as if the connection had been broken by the slow pressure of a finger. I said hello twice again, just to be sure, and hung up. Doubtless someone had dialed a wrong number. But why not say so?

I hiked up the stairs, on my way to the bedroom to get into something loose. At the landing, out of sight of the floor below, I heard the front door open and guessed it was Judith. The kitchen door creaked open and Judith's voice greeted Mirabelle.

"Any messages, Mirabelle?"

"Well, lemme see. Couple of people sellin' things. And, oh yeah, yeah, some man called. Asked when you'd be home and I said 'bout two. Said he'd call back."

Indifferently Judith said, "Didn't he leave his name?"

"Yeah. Lessee."

A pause. I waited on the landing.

"Stanton," Mirabelle said. "Richard Stanton."

I froze. Richard Stanton—the name Ridge Standish had used at The Hacienda! Something that sounded like a package thudded to the floor downstairs.

It was a moment before Judith's voice, hushed and tremulous, floated thinly up the stairs. "Did . . . did he leave a number?"

"No, ma'm."

I crept to the bedroom and silently shut the door, noticing that I left a smear of sweat on the knob. The full shock of the name hit me as I mechanically slipped off my tie. It must have been Standish who had hung up only a few minutes before. He had expected Judith to be at home but assumed I'd be at the office. Why, on the previous call, had he risked leaving his name? But of course it was not his real name, simply a code name that he knew Judith would instantly recognize. He had to have thought that, even if I heard it, it would be meaningless to me.

I considered that as I dropped clothes onto the bed. If he thought the name Richard Stanton had no significance to me, only one conclusion could be drawn: Judith had never told him about Gus Klein tracking them down at The Hacienda, never mentioned the existence of the incriminating pictures, let alone that I had confronted her with them. If she had, he would then have known that the Richard Stanton alias also had been revealed. Probably Judith had withheld the information in fear that he would flee to avoid involvement in such a messy situation.

Judith had seen the red Porsche in the garage, so she knew I was home. Probably she was now fretting over whether I had heard her conversation with Mirabelle. I pulled on dark-blue slacks and a loose-fitting white shirt and trod heavily down the stairs. Judith stood at a front window in a patch of sunlight, back toward me, hands clamped around her shoulders. Despite my noisy approach, she didn't turn around until I said "Hi." Then she whirled as if struck by a spasm.

Her features appeared bunched together, as though from intense concentration. She made an effort to relax them.

"Hi. I didn't hear you." Then, as if her words were

some sort of giveaway: "I was thinking about the yard. It needs a clean-up. I'll get after the gardener." She strolled to the table in front of the sofa, got a cigarette and lit it. "How did things go today?"

"The usual." I felt a sudden compulsion to unnerve her. "Speaking of phone calls . . ." I paused, reaching in my pocket for a cigarette and taking my time lighting it.

Her breasts rose under her lime-colored dress as she held her breath.

"I got an odd one," I said, "just before you came in."

Her face drained of color. She blew smoke out slowly from between stiffened lips.

"The phone rang and I picked it up. I gave my name. I heard the sound of breathing."

I left it at that until she was forced to say, in a strained voice, "Well, what happened?"

"Nothing. Nothing at all. I asked who was calling. There was a click and the connection was broken."

"Just a wrong number," she said quickly. "It happens all the time."

"Probably. But it made me think of those prowlers we'd once been bothered with."

She blew out smoke in an agitated burst. "Now why would you think of that?"

"I've heard that some thieves telephone a house to find out if anyone's home. If they don't get an answer, they bust in and help themselves."

"Dan, you *are* imagining things."

"Apparently I didn't think I was imagining things when I got that gun."

Her jaw set angrily. *"Please.* Let's not go into that again. I told you how I feel about guns in the house."

I ignored her. "Obviously we must both have been damned scared. Why else would I have called a private detective agency?"

The cigarette broke in her fingers. Bending down, her face hidden, she ground out the remains in the ash tray.

As if not comprehending, she choked out, "Private detective agency"—neither a question nor a statement.

"Yes. Funny thing. Just before the accident I'd written some phone numbers on my calendar pad at the office. Nancy Mercer, my secretary, happened to save them. One number was unfamiliar to her and of course to me. So I had Nancy call it, out of curiosity. It was for a private detective agency."

Judith swayed slightly and flopped down on the sofa. Controlling her voice, she said, "Did you speak to them?"

"No. As soon as Nancy told me who the number was for, I knew it must have been about the prowlers. Evidently I didn't put much faith in the local police."

I could feel her relief as though it was expanding inside my own body.

"Yes," she said eagerly, "now I do remember you mentioning it. What was their name?"

I was getting on dangerous ground. "I don't think Nancy mentioned the name. Just a detective agency. I threw the calendar page away."

Judith lit another cigarette and exhaled a long plume of smoke.

"But I wondered why I had their number on the calendar on December twenty-ninth. You said the prowler business happened more than a year ago. That was months before that date."

She took another long drag, letting the smoke drift from her mouth. "Yes. But then we had a recurrence—right after Christmas. That's when you decided the local police weren't enough."

I sat down on the arm of the sofa, away from her. "Strange that Jeb didn't mention the second occurrence."

She gave me a hard, calculating look, as though considering if she was being baited. "We were afraid people might think we were having pipe dreams if we mentioned the second episode. So we decided not to tell anyone."

I turned the screw a little tighter. "Except the detective agency."

Her voice broke with impatience. "Yes, except the detective agency."

I affected solicitude. "You sound upset, Judith. Are you still nervous about prowlers?"

Unthinkingly she burst out: "Well, of course I'm nervous about them! Who wouldn't be! This lonely place . . ."

"Then perhaps I'd better replace that gun. I'm sure it can be easily arranged."

A trapped expression darted across her face. She changed direction. "No," she said petulantly, "it isn't the prowlers that make me nervous. It's you talking, talking, talking about them!"

"I'm sorry. It all started with that strange phone call.

Maybe, whoever it was called earlier, while we were both out." I got up and took a step toward the kitchen. "I'll ask Mirabelle."

"No!"

I turned and looked at her with exaggerated surprise. Her whole body tensed but she managed a meager smile.

"I already asked Mirabelle about any calls. There were only a couple and they were from salesmen."

As if she had heard her name, Mirabelle ambled out from the kitchen and went to the closet for her hat. Judith rushed to her, babbling something about groceries and cleaning supplies. A horn beeped outside. "My taxi," Mirabelle said. Judith hustled her out the door, closed it with a bang, and sped back to the hall table stacked with the packages she had brought in.

Without a glance into the living room, she said, "I must put these away," and ran up the stairs.

I slid down on the sofa cushion and looked up at the ceiling, listening to Judith's footsteps repeatedly criss-crossing the floor. She was not just putting away her purchases. She was worrying about those phone calls, worrying about the detective agency, worrying about the gun, perhaps even worrying about whether my memory was coming back. In short, she was worrying that her whole carefully organized life was once more in jeopardy.

Was it pure meanness that had made me push her so far? Not entirely. I also wanted to panic her into some impetuous action that would decisively establish her guilt. I was uneasily aware that I had increased her distrust of me.

The footsteps on the floor above stopped. In about ten minutes Judith came back downstairs. She wore fresh makeup and an attitude of poised aloofness.

"I'm going to the drug store," she said. "I forgot to pick up a prescription."

I looked up from a magazine. "Prescription? Nothing wrong, is there?"

She bit her lip. "Just something for the nerves. I'll be back shortly."

She stalked out the door.

It was apparent that Judith could use a tranquilizer. But perhaps it also provided an excuse to make a phone call. She must be eaten with curiosity as to where Standish was when he called. Could she have thought—incredible!—that he had checked into The Hacienda? After all, if Judith had not told him of their exposure by camera, Standish might still feel safe in using the name Richard Stanton. I looked up the number of the motel and called. There was no Richard Stanton registered, nor was he expected.

I had another phone call to make. Gus Klein should be told that Ridge Standish had attempted to contact Judith.

"The crazy son of a bitch," Klein said when I told him. "Why would he want to open up that jar of bees again?"

I said what had been nagging at my mind all along. "I can't help feeling that Standish was in it with my wife—trying to kill me. Alibi or no alibi. He got off scot free. After all this time, perhaps he thinks it's safe to try again."

"You got some new information?"

I decided to leave Ginnie completely out of it. "No. As I say, it's just a feeling."

I heard him suck his teeth. "You'd be smart to have me put a tail on your wife."

The suggestion was repugnant but it made sense. Obviously, I couldn't follow Judith around.

"Go ahead and do it."

"Okay. And we should bug that phone."

I felt the world tightening around me. "Go ahead. When can you do it?"

"The quicker the better. Tell you what. Take her out to dinner tonight. Leave a key under the mat. Then I can come in like a real little gentleman. Call me if she won't go out. If I don't hear from you I'll telephone about seven-thirty. No answer and I come in."

"Alright," I said resignedly. "Anything else?"

"One thing. Where'll you go to dinner?"

"I have no idea."

"Great little place up on 101. Called The Hacienda. Very discriminating clientele."

His arid chuckle came down the wire as if rubbing over a nutmeg grater.

As I hung up and stood there wincing, the phone rang. It was Ginnie, asking for Judith. She spoke with cool politeness, the way a well-bred woman would talk to a waiter. Embarrassment and guilt swept over me as my mind flashed images of us on the kitchen floor, the declaration of love accompanied by the indictment of Judith, Ginnie's wounded pride and her curt dismissal of me.

"Judith telephoned earlier," Ginnie said. "I'm just returning her call."

"Judith's not home." I hesitated, then told her about calling Gus Klein and his plan for keeping Judith under surveillance.

For a moment she didn't answer. Then, as if the problem were mine alone: "Well, good luck."

Finality was in her goodbye. It was obvious that Ginnie intended to disassociate herself from the night before as well as from whatever we had shared in my blacked-out past. My conscience eased.

Judith, I was sure, would welcome having dinner out; anything to avoid being cooped up with me. That sparked a thought: Why not give the bugged phone a chance to work over the weekend?

I called Jeb and arranged a golf date for the next morning, Saturday.

14

I got back from my golf game with Jeb in mid-afternoon. Judith was not at home. I took a long, hot shower, changed into fresh sports clothes and came back downstairs. Still no Judith.

I looked at the phone, a thought forming in my mind. By the time I strolled out by the pool and came back, the thought was a decision. I dialed Gus Klein's number. As expected, I got an answering service. The girl melodically gave me a number where Klein could be reached.

When he answered my ring, I apologized for bothering him on Saturday.

"Hell, I'm a batch. Nothing to bother. Besides, I wanted to call you but I was afraid I'd get the missus. We got something. Hold on."

I sat down on a small chair and looked uneasily at our front door. If Judith should suddenly walk in . . . but no, I'd hear the car first.

Klein came back on. "Listen to this. It's a tape recording. We got it off your phone less than an hour ago. Obviously you were out. Ready?"

I clamped the receiver to my ear and told him to go ahead. I heard the punch of a button followed by a whirring, scratching sound. Then:

(Judith's voice): "Hello."

(A brisk, woman's voice): "Is this Judith Marriott of one-fourteen Summit Way, Kentwood?"

"Yes, it is."

"This is the telegraph office in San Rafael."

"Yes?"

"We have a telegram for you. Our instructions are to speak only to you and suggest that you come to our office and pick up the message personally."

There was a scratchy pause. I felt my hand trying to crush the receiver and imagined Judith had been doing the same. Finally, in a voice straining for control, Judith said:

"Read it to me."

There was a faint rustle of paper.

"This is the message: 'Unable to reach you on phone without interference. Imperative I see you. Will come to San Francisco next week. Write me care of General Delivery San Diego stating time and place we can meet. Stanton.' "

There was a long silence. Sweat prickled on my back.

"Are you there?"

(Judith, breath strangling her voice): "Yes. Where was the message sent from?"

"Ensenada, Mexico. It was sent at one-ten today."

"Thank you. I'll be down to pick it up." *Bang.*

Again the whirring scratch of the tape. A snap as Klein turned it off.

After the thin, tinny sound of the voices, Klein's burst into my ear as though he were standing next to me and shouting.

"Stanton—I mean Standish—is either a goddam fool or the world's bravest man, or both. He's got to know he's wanted for embezzlement. My God, it was in all the papers—well, the New York papers anyway—seven months ago. I can only think of one goddam explanation."

My mind was still reeling from what I had heard on the tape.

"Maybe not a good explanation but it's just crazy enough to be right. I figure that Standish either couldn't cash in those securities, or he did and then pissed away the money, or was robbed. He's bottled up in Ensenada and he's desperate."

I remembered driving down to Ensenada from San Clemente with Judith. A crowded resort and fishing port. A good place to hide out, particularly now during the tourist season.

"He must figure that if she writes him in San Diego—that's not too far from Ensenada—and agrees to meet him, she must still be carrying the same old torch. So maybe he's decided to hop up here and finish the job your wife almost did last January one. Then she'll get your dough, including your insurance, and they'll be off to live happily ever after. I said it's crazy, but goddam it, we've got to consider it."

"It's always nice to get good news," I said wryly. I felt a tingling numbness at the back of my neck. Klein's theory *did* add up. Now I knew why Judith was not at home. She had written an answer to Standish and was out posting it, picking up the telegram along the way and destroying it.

"Got any advice?" I said.

"I got you down for two choices. One, you get yourself a lawyer, like right now, and file for divorce. You've got all the evidence you need to get her on adultery; no, *I've* got it—the pictures. But there's a couple big holes in that one. Your wife could contest it and get a jury trial. And she might just come out smellin' like a rose. She could say she was crazy in love with you but you gave her the icy treatment, so she was powerless when this other guy gave her the seduction routine. And she could back up that love crap by pointing out that, after the accident, she saved your life, then stuck by you when you were going through all that sawbones bit. That's hole number one. Here's hole number two: those two might get you killed before you even had time to file papers."

There was a third hole, I thought. If Judith instituted a countersuit, her lawyer would surely hire an investigator and perhaps find out about Ginnie. Not only would the adulteries cancel each other, there would be more notoriety than ever. And I couldn't win.

"Too many holes," I said. "What's the second choice?"

"Okay. I think you better assume you're a setup for a hit. So here's what I'd do in your spot. Go see the Sheriff, Bogano, and give him the whole schmeer, including the wiretap info that just burned your ears."

"Oh God, no!"

"Why not? You're a taxpayer in that county. Bogano owes you something. That's why better it should come from you, not me. But you can bet Bogano'll have me on the horn soon's you've stepped out. So you're afraid Bogano will blab it around. Well, you've just got to take that chance. I know Sal and I'll ask him to sign in blood that he'll keep his mouth shut. I'm betting he will, especially now that you could be a sitting duck."

"He'll think the accident scrambled my brains."

"The hell he will. He already has more than a sneaking suspicion your old lady got away with murder. That bothers Sal. He'd like to prove he was right. You're gonna find him a very attentive audience. He'll see you get some protection. And I'll be doing my bit, too."

"I'll think about it."

"Not too long." Klein paused. "And don't mention the embezzlement caper. I'm not even telling Whitley that Standish has turned up. Not yet. If I did, he'd hit the panic button and the insurance dicks, the Feds, God knows who else would join the party. The San Diego post office would be like cops' convention. Standish would take one look and he'd be off and running."

I heard the sound of wheels crunching up the driveway. "I've got to get off. My wife's just driving in."

"Act normal. Treat her like she was Snow White."

Too late for that, I thought. My needling had surely aroused her suspicions about my motives.

"I got a man lives in Tijuana who's checking on Standish. We may be able to nab him when he drops into the P.O. for the letter. That'll mean a bonus—the reward money for the embezzlement charge."

I heard the car door slam.

". . . and you *will* see Bogano?"

"Yes," I said wearily, "I'll see Bogano."

I was on the stairs, pretending to be just coming down, as Judith pushed through the door hugging a grocery bag. The pretense was wasted. She sailed past me into the kitchen, scarcely muttering a word of greeting.

A few minutes later she came out to where I was sitting in a director's chair beside the pool. Her face was drawn and she was massaging one temple with her fingertips.

"I've got a splitting headache. I'm going up and crawl into bed."

I commiserated briefly. "Anything I can bring you?"

"No, I'll take aspirin and bring up some magazines."

"Magazines," I said, a thought striking me. "I've read them all. I think I'll go pick up a couple of paperbacks as long as we're staying home."

This time she gave no sign of suspicion. She nodded painfully and left me. I had no doubt her headache was real.

Now I'd get my part over with, I'd see Sheriff Bogano.

After I had told my story, Sheriff Bogano leaned far back in his swivel chair, brown shirted belly stretched to a slight curve. He picked reflectively at his teeth with a match cover.

"You're sure that message really came from the telegraph office?"

I fidgeted on the metal chair. "I didn't check it out, if that's what you mean. But why would I question it?"

Bogano's chair made a loud grinding noise as he swung forward and picked up his phone. "It's easy to check it," he said, dialing a number.

I had told Bogano the full story of Judith's affair with Ridge Standish. Omitted was Standish's flight from a felony, my relationship with Ginnie and some of the background information she had provided. None of it was necessary to the case against the two I hoped to entrap.

"Hello, Charley. Sal Bogano here. I understand you received a telegram earlier today for a Judith Marriott in Kentwood."

Bogano waited, eyeing me over the telephone.

"Thanks, Charley. She lost it. I said I'd get her another copy. Mrs. Marriott is a friend of mine . . . Charley, that's fine. I'll stop by shortly and get it."

I was relieved to find that Bogano was acting discreetly.

"So," he said to me, hanging up. "You heard. Right now I don't think your wife is feeling very good."

"She's in bed with a bad headache."

"Mr. Marriott, I think your wife's got a headache as bad as anyone can get." He tugged at his big chin and gave a wry little smile. "I guess I made it pretty clear I never did feel right about that accident. It bugs the hell out of me the things some people get away with. Maybe, like most citizens, you think people don't get away with murder. Well, they do. It happens all the time. Sometimes it's a drunk who falls asleep in his car in the garage and leaves the motor running—his wife says. Sometimes it's a woman with a bad heart who trips on a busted stair, or who needs medicine fast and isn't given it. Sometimes it's a professional job that looks like a freak accident." He raised his thick eyebrows at me. "And sometimes it's a car skidding off the road and crashing down a mountainside."

Bogano leaned on his desk like a giant bust carved in bronze. His face, under the folds of flesh, projected an iron determination. He was not, I thought, simply a dedicated civil servant. He was a zealot.

"Some of them are murders," he said. "We know damned well they're murders—but we don't have one little bit of evidence to work on." His eyes fixed on mine. "This time, Mr. Marriott, we've got some warning. You've done the right thing coming in here. We'll do everything we can. But there's only so much we *can* do; we've got a lot of territory to cover. Are you keeping on Gus Klein?"

"I thought I would."

"That's smart. Klein's a good man. A little old fashioned, some people think. But I like that. He's experienced, and he's got guts."

"Is there anything I should be doing?"

"No. Just go about as usual, and act as natural as you can with your wife. Oh, there *is* one thing. Call Klein and ask him to let me borrow those film strips."

I felt a wave of shame. "Is that necessary, Sheriff? Isn't it enough that you know about them?"

He shook his head, the cloud of hair bouncing. "I don't plan to show it at the local movie house. But I want to make a blowup of Standish's face. It will be done in our lab. I'll mask off the rest of the film so that no one, not even our technician, will see your wife. Just Standish. I *do* have to know what the suspect looks like."

15

Nothing more developed until just before five on Monday. I was in the office, having decided to start working full time (if only to be free of Judith), when Gus Klein was announced from the reception lobby.

Hurrying in, looking worn and gray, he slumped into a chair.

"Just back from San Diego," he said. "We got zilch—Standish didn't show."

I sat down behind my desk. "Perhaps there wasn't any letter. I only *guessed* my wife answered Standish's telegram."

"Oh, there was a letter. I'll give you the scenario. I took off for San Diego before six this morning. I had blowups of Standish's picture, eight by tens, that I got from Bogano—yeah, I loaned him the film strips like you said. My Tijuana guy had crossed the border and I met him in San Diego before the post office opened. Incidentally, he'd made a quick check on Standish in Ensenada and turned up zero. Anyway . . ."

Klein stopped and looked out the window, his face suddenly stamped with guilt.

"Mr. Marriott, I'm afraid I committed a crime in your behalf. Before going down, I'd faked some credentials using the name Richard Stanton. The minute that post office opened I was at one of the windows flashing the phony identification. I stayed in the post office so as not to miss Standish while my Tijuana buddy hustled the letter down the street. He steamed it open and made a photocopy. He'd set that up in advance. He was back in less than ten minutes. I stayed out of sight while he went to the window—different than the one I'd gone to—and handed back the letter, sealed. He said he'd found it on the sidewalk, that somebody must have dropped it. The clerk took it back without any questions."

I was half out of my chair. "The letter—what did it say?"

Klein reached into a bulging inside pocket that was practically an office and pulled out the folded photocopy. "Here, read it yourself. But maybe you should be ready with a stiff drink. You got a shock coming."

I spread the crisp paper out on the desk. The letter was in Judith's handwriting.

Dear Ridge,

As you might guess, I was very surprised to hear from you.

It's too bad we couldn't have talked, because what I would have had to say would probably persuade you not to come up here. As you know, about eight months ago Dan and I were in a horrible accident. Dan nearly died and, until recently, has been in a hospital undergoing surgery and treatment for loss of memory. It has been a terrible time for both of us.

But terrible as it has been, the ordeal has had one worthwhile result. It brought my husband and me together again.

I wouldn't want to do anything that might compromise my relationship with Dan. On the other hand, your telegram says it's "imperative" that you see me, which implies that you are in some kind of trouble. Certainly I don't want to deny you any help I can give.

If this is the case, and you still wish to see me despite what I have written, I'll be glad to meet you. But I think it unwise that we take any chance of being seen together.

Here's what I'll do. On Wednesday I'll drive out to The Mountain House, a bar and restaurant about six miles up from where we live. Anyone can direct you. I'll be there at 5 P.M. and will meet you in the parking lot.

Ridge, I beg you not to come unless the matter is extremely urgent.

Judith

Looking up, I could feel myself gaping at Klein.

"Oh, she's a sly one," he said. "Even though Standish ran out on her once, she's probably still got hot pants for him. She wants to see him but she's scared to write anything that would give him a chance to blackmail her or that would look bad if you somehow got wind of it. So she lards it all with the true-blue-to-hubby stuff, so's that if you should ever see it you'll not only let her off the hook but think she's made in heaven. She's got it both ways— she invites Standish to come up and at the same time avoids incriminating herself if something goes haywire."

"Any idea what happened to Standish?"

"Could be he decided it was too much of a risk. Anyway, come three o'clock, I decided I better get the hell back here, leaving my buddy to mind the store. I checked in with Bogano and there's nothing new. Also, I called my office. The phone bug hadn't picked up anything interesting."

"I just can't believe Standish would take all these chances when he knows he's wanted for grand theft."

"I say he's broke or damned close to it and he's desperate. Your wife could solve his problem. Tell me, Mr. Marriott, if you'll excuse the nosiness, how much are you worth, counting the insurance?"

I made a rough calculation. "I'd say close to half a million dollars, two hundred thousand in insurance."

Klein whistled through his teeth. "Well, now, I'd say a jackpot like that would move a guy like Standish to gamble. He might not like the odds but they're probably not much worse than what he'd be up against sitting on his rosy in Ensenada."

We looked up as Nancy Mercer appeared in the door.

"Excuse me, but there's a call for Mr. Klein from San

Diego. A Mr. Luis Arguello and he says it's urgent. It's on my line."

Klein slapped his knee. "That's my Tijuana guy. He must've called my office. I told 'em I'd be here."

I pushed a button and handed him my phone.

Klein announced himself, then listened, his gray face sharp with interest. "When was that? . . . Hmm . . . Yeah, I see . . . Okay, I'll handle it up here."

Hanging up, Klein waggled his eyebrows at me. "Standish pulled it off! He got the letter. Talk about a slippery article!"

"You mean your man didn't recognize him?"

"Standish was probably in disguise. We'd factored that in as a possible, but he made it anyway. So it looks like Mr. Ridge Standish will be paying your wife that visit. Unless he gets collared en route, which I doubt. I've got a lot of faith in that con man."

Chilling as the thought was, I felt a hard satisfaction. At last things might be coming to a head. I handed the photocopy back to Klein and asked how he planned to handle it.

"I'll be at The Mountain House before she is. She doesn't know me, so I'm covered. If Standish shows, I'll give him plenty of rope—just keep a tail on him. *And* your wife. I'll get Bogano to patrol the road in case I miss. Unmarked cars. Then we'll play it by ear until we see what Standish and your wife are up to."

After having tried and convicted Judith in my office, I was more astonished than ever by what awaited me at home. Judith greeted me at the door clad in black silk hostess pajamas, hair sleekly combed, makeup perfect and, even more puzzling, a smile that was radiant.

She threw her arms around my neck and planted a lingering kiss on my mouth. I stood there as unresponsive as a dummy, feeling like the idiot husband in a television situation comedy.

"Come in and relax," she said, helping me off with my suit coat.

I mumbled something incoherent and followed her awkwardly into the living room. The lights were soft, an unseasonal fire crackled, and a frosted pitcher of martinis flanked by two glasses sat on the coffee table.

"I feel wonderful," Judith said, loosening my tie and pulling me down beside her on the sofa.

I recalled the headache she complained about on Saturday, persisting, or so she said, through Sunday.

"Oh," I said foolishly, "no more headache?"

"No more headache," she said, smiling at me as she handed me a drink.

She took a sip of her own and added, "Lately, I've been feeling awful. Just a delayed reaction to everything, I guess. Oh, Dan, I know I've been miserable to live with. But I'm going to make it all up to you. You'll see."

I felt as though I had dreamed my conversation with Gus Klein.

"You *have* been rather distant," I said, hoping to draw her out. Immediately I regretted the words; they sounded like an invitation to be otherwise.

Apparently she interpreted them that way. She snuggled

her head against my shoulder, careful to avoid mussing her hair, and stroked my arm. I remained still for a moment, then released myself by reaching for a cigarette. She took one, too, and I held the match for her.

She let the subject drop, as if aware that her attitude had changed much too abruptly to seem plausible. But her vivacity remained undimmed as she asked about the office and reported the trivia of the day. I had the illusion that we were an old married couple comfortably accustomed to exchanging every thought and experience.

Half way through the second martini, with the tension relaxed, she returned to her self-criticism.

"I guess I've been brooding about my telling you . . . how *estranged* we'd been before the accident. It must have had you thinking all sorts of terrible things." She looked down at her lap like a chastened child. "And I guess a lot of your thoughts were true. There was really no excuse for the way I acted but I was feeling so alone and sorry for myself."

I was beginning to see what she was up to.

"I began to resent you for what I *imagined* you were thinking. That's really why I've been so nervous and bitchy." She put her hand on my knee. "But everything's new and different now. Let's forget the past."

I felt my mouth give a tight smile. "Forget the past? That's exactly my problem."

"I'm sorry. But you know what I mean."

I did. Fearful of what I might know or imagine about her, she was trying to soften the impact by offering a mild concession to the truth. She attributed her unspecified acts to a confused, forlorn woman, one who bore not the slightest resemblance to the present Judith. She had completely reformed, and if I had an ounce of compassion I would ignore anything unfavorably connected with the wife she had been. Her story was an amplification of the one she had told me after we first arrived home and I learned we had occupied separate rooms. Then she was attempting to forestall trouble. Now it had arrived.

"Dan, remember the glorious time we had at San Clemente? Just the two of us? Why don't we chuck everything and go away?"

"Go away? Hell, Judith, I've only been back in the office a little over a week."

She filled our glasses and waited until I drank some.

"I mean go away for good." She gulped half her drink and refilled the glass. "Sell the house, quit your job. There are plenty of other good places to live. Plenty of other good jobs. Besides, money is no problem. We can leave all these associations behind us." Her finger drew a line on my thigh.

Now everything was clear. Whatever attraction Standish might still hold for her, it was balanced by her distrust of him. And she must still harbor bitterness for his flight during a crisis. If she could deny me access to the evidence against her, remove me from the scenes that invited recall, she could afford to avoid murder. She had approached murder once and knew the terror of its touch. She wanted, above all, security. Perhaps she was at last accepting the truth that she was no longer young.

"I'm sorry, Judith. We can't do it."

She pouted. "Why not? Give me one good reason why not."

"All right. A selfish one. I believe if I'm ever to get back my memory, it will be here, surrounded by familiar things."

Her face seemed to darken. She swirled her drink rapidly. "And that's the only reason?"

I looked at her levelly. "Could there be any other?"

She squirmed and sat up straight. She gnawed at her underlip, her breath quickening. Then she burst out with: "Oh, goddam it all, let's stop playing games. Ever since we came back home, you've been wondering what kind of woman I was. Well, I've told you and I've told you *why*. What do you want me to do to prove myself?"

I was silent, not knowing what to say.

She sprang to her feet, spilling some of her drink, downing what was left. "Is it because I've been the frigid wife lately? Is that what's eating you up? Did you think I was just faking it all at the beach cottage?"

"No, I didn't, Judith."

She bent down, lurching against the table, and splashed another drink into her glass. It was apparent she had been drinking before I arrived. I lit a cigarette, watching her as she swayed above me, draining her glass. I wondered if I was being sanctimonious in my judgment of her—after all, I too had been guilty of adultery. But there were differences. Ginnie, as far as I knew, had been my only extramarital experience; Standish had been for Judith the culmination of a long career of promiscuity. I had decided on divorce; Judith, I believed, had tried to kill me.

Judith took a shaky step backward. She held the empty glass loosely upside down, then let it slip to the floor. Her eyes blazed at me.

"What kind of woman d'you want? Some bloodless little mouse like Ginnie Scott?"

I jerked to the edge of the sofa. Did she know? But I could see it was pure nastiness.

"No, I don't." I realized I meant it.

She wasn't listening. "Or d'you want a *real* woman, a woman like this . . ."

She fumbled with the top button of her silk pajama jacket. She gave an impatient shake of her head, flinging out her dark hair. Then she grabbed her jacket where the collar met and ripped viciously downward. There was a rough, rending sound. Cloth buttons popped and spun to the floor. She stood there naked above the waist, the torn top clutched in her fist like a black rebel flag. She flung it to the floor.

"Isn't this what you want?" She cupped her breasts in her hands, moved forward, bent slightly, and held them just above my eyes. The nipples were like hard little rosettes, signalling a passion aroused by her own frenzy.

I stubbed out my cigarette, looking down at the ash tray. "Judith, for God's sake . . ."

"And this?"

I looked up. She had stepped back and was tearing off the bottoms. They stuck at her ankles and she bent down and yanked them over each high heel. She balled them up and tossed them across the room.

She caressed her shoulders, then raised her hands and clasped them behind her neck. She swayed toward me.

"Isn't this what you want? Isn't this what you always wanted?"

I stood up. A thought leaped snarling into my mind: She was offering to barter her body for an acquiescence that would permit her to refrain from murder. The realization quenched any desire I might have felt.

She dropped her hands and lightly stroked her hips. Wriggling close, she reached out and started to tug at my top shirt button. I pulled away, suddenly angry.

"Goddam it, Judith, you think sex is the solution to everything!"

She stopped as though I'd struck her. For an instant a bewildered look crossed her face and her shoulders slumped. Then her chin came up, she straightened, and I had the odd impression of staring at the haughty, unreal figure of a model in a fashion magazine.

Her voice dripped venom: "You poor, poor son of a bitch."

Somehow maintaining an air of icy dignity, she pivoted on her heel, almost strutted to her ripped pajamas, kneeled down and picked them up. She walked gracefully to the hall and glided up the stairs, head high, like a princess approaching her coronation. I flopped wearily back on the sofa, lit another cigarette and contemplated what remained in the martini pitcher. I finished it off, then went to the kitchen and made a fresh batch. Coming back to the sofa, I sat there smoking and drinking, watching the fire die.

Two hours must have passed before I finally mounted the stairs. I was quite drunk and had only a blurred impression of standing in front of Judith's door. I wondered fuzzily if she was still awake and what my reception would be.

The wondering stopped when I turned the knob. The door was locked.

So once again I was to sleep in the long vacant adjoining room. We had come full circle.

And we had come to the point where Judith, in concert with Ridge Standish, must proceed to the final solution.

16

Judith was still in her room when I left for the office on Tuesday. That was the only relief I knew all day. The rest was one long, jittery wait, of fumbling with papers, staring blindly at reports, mumbling evasive answers to questions I did not really hear. One more day, I kept thinking, one more day and perhaps I would know what my fate was to be. Constantly I eyed the telephone, hoping for some word that might reveal Standish's next move.

By three o'clock my patience was exhausted. I called Gus Klein. He was out and was expected back at four-thirty.

He called me at quarter to five and was his usual loquacious self.

"I was following your wife. Man, does she like to spend your money. I had a tour of S.F.'s better stores—Magnin's, City of Paris, Saks, you name it. Anyway, I left her about forty minutes ago after seeing her safely home. Undetected, I hope."

It surprised me that Judith had not stayed home, in case of a call. "Anything suspicious?"

Klein pondered the question with a growling throat noise. "Can't be sure. Going into the city, she cut off the highway and went by way of Sausalito."

"Sausalito?"

"Oh yeah, your memory. Well, Sausalito's a little town about ten minutes from the Bridge, below 101 on the Bay. Loaded with swingers. I followed her down the main drag, past the town, and she turned into the parking lot at Ziggie's. That's a booze and rock joint next to the water. She walks in the front door. I wait a minute, then do the same. No Judith Marriott. I wait awhile, thinking maybe she's powdering her nose. No show. Well, there's a big deck outside where people eat and drink, and to the left there's steps leading down to a walkway that brings you back again to the street. I take that and come back to the parking lot. Her T-Bird's still there. I hate to admit it but I'm baffled. If I go looking for her, she's sure to come back to the car and take off out of sight. The only thing to do is wait in my car and keep an eye on hers. That I do. In about ten minutes, she comes out Ziggie's front door, gets in her car and drives into town. She was gone maybe twenty minutes."

"How about the phone booth?"

"No, I checked that. But there's a boat and tackle shop across from the back steps and a slug of other joints just down the line. She could've gone into any one of 'em and phoned." I heard a voice calling in the background. "Hold on a minute," he said to me.

When he came back on, his voice grated with suppressed excitement. "Our bug has been sounding off again.

A call was picked up on your phone at two-ten this afternoon. Your wife was in town then. Your cleaning woman took the call. I won't play the tape. I'll talk it."

My hand shook as I picked up a pencil to make notes.

"Mirabelle tells the Voice that your missus is out and she doesn't know when she'll be back. The Voice asks her to take a message. Now this should blow your brain. Here it is, taken from the transcript that was just handed to me:

'Will you please write this down?'

'Yessir, I got a pencil.'

'This is Mr. Stanton. Please cancel meeting˒ for four P.M. tomorrow. Got that?'

'Yessir. Four P.M. Cancel meetin' place.'

'Now this may sound odd but Mrs. Marriott will understand. Ready?'

'Yessir.'

'Please check Palgrave.'

'Whassat?'

'Palgrave. P-a-l-g-r-a-v-e.'

'Got it.'

'Please check Palgrave. Page two five six, last four lines. Got it?'

'Two five six, last four lines.'

'Right. Now write this down: Use that instead of your first idea. Keep the timing constant.'

'Okay. You sure Mrs. Marriott's gonna know what this is all about?'

'Yes, I'm sure. I teach writing. It has to do with a story Mrs. Marriott's working on.'

'Ohhh, I get you.' "

Gus Klein had been half mimicking the imagined voices.
Now he said normally, "That's it. And don't ask me what
the hell it means."

I finished with my notes. "Palgrave's *Golden Treasury,*"
I said. "It's a book of poems—English poets. I noticed a
copy of it at home."

"Never heard of it. Okay, I'll send my gal out to the
library. Whatever it says in this guy Palgrave's book, you
can be goddamned sure it will take some unravelling. Oh,
that Standish, he's a cute one. If I figure it out, I'll let you
know. Ditto with you. I suppose you'll be getting the
book?"

"As soon as you hang up."

"I'm *hung* up."

I sent Nancy Mercer to the library for a copy. She was
back in half an hour and placed a small, battered volume
on my desk.

I flipped to page two fifty-six. The poem was Shelley's
"Stanza Written in Dejection Near Naples." I read all of
the last stanza in order to evaluate the last four lines in
context:

> "Yet now despair itself is mild
> Even as the winds and waters are;
> I could lie down like a tired child,
> And weep away the life of care
> Which I have borne, and yet must bear,—
> Till death like sleep might steal on me,
> And I might feel in the warm air

My cheek grow cold, and hear the sea
Breathe o'er my dying brain its last monotony."

I studied the last four lines, comprehending Shelley but not Standish. Two thoughts stood out—death and the sea. My God, were they planning to drown me! But no, the phone message referred not to me but to a rendezvous. Standish had cancelled The Mountain House as the place for the meeting. But he had not changed the time: On the phone he had said, "Keep the timing constant." Where did that leave me? Suddenly it seemed obvious—Judith was to meet him someplace by the sea—a place he must have assumed she knew about—and there they would decide on the manner of my death. I saw my hand tremble on the page.

I called Gus Klein.

"I just finished reading it," he said. "Sad goddamned thing, huh?"

"Maybe you don't know *how* sad."

"You mean you got it figured out?"

I told him my interpretation.

"Well, yeah, that could be it. Anyway it looks like Standish is taking no chances—he *thinks*."

"Do you think you should notify Whitley at this point?"

"You're asking me am I crazy. Whitley'd have a posse up here and queer the whole bit. No. Mr. Marriott, I'll handle this solo. I'll just tag along after your wife and if Standish shows, I'll nab them together. I'll call Bogano and tell him the mountain meeting is off, and will ask him to stand by just in case. But this looks like a job for a loner. That's me."

When I got home that night, Judith was again in her room. I had a couple of drinks, ate dinner from a can and went to bed early with one of the paperbacks I had bought. I read about fifty pages, comprehending nothing. At nine-thirty I took a sleeping pill, turned off the light and in about half an hour dozed off. I slept fitfully, plagued by nightmarish dreams, awakening often to hear the soft creaking of footsteps on the other side of the bathroom. The last time I looked at my watch it was almost three A.M. Judith was still pacing the floor.

Awakening on the fateful Wednesday morning, I downed an instant breakfast and left early to make sure of avoiding Judith. The routine in the office was a repetition of the day before, only more so. By three-thirty I felt like a candidate for the psycho ward. I contemplated the pile of cigarette butts in the ash tray and said to myself, *My God, I've got to DO something!*

I called Gus Klein. I had not, of course, expected to find him in. I was right. It was just something to do. I sat smoking for another ten minutes. Then I stood up and muttered aloud, "The hell with *this!*"

I started out the door, stopped, came back, picked up the phone and dialed. When the girl's voice answered, I asked her to tell Gus Klein that I expected to be home around five.

I drove the Porsche along the Embarcadero, past the great steamship piers, on my way to the Golden Gate Bridge. A misty fog had blown in, becoming thick and drippy as I reached the toll plaza. I started the windshield wipers and turned on the headlights. I drove slowly across the Bridge, gripping the wheel tightly against the stiff wind whirling in through the Gate. As I came off on the opposite shore, huge banks of fog climbed heavily over the backs of the sharp-ridge hills and gale gusts lashed at the car. In the iodine-colored light from the highway lamps, I saw a sign reading "Sausalito turnoff, 1/4 mile." Deciding it would be less hazardous down there, I took the turnoff. The road rolled and twisted down the almost perpendicular hills, levelling off only when it reached the water. There it straightened out into a narrow street running parallel to the Bay. The fog was less dense here but visibility extended for only about fifty feet. Ahead, a faint glow marked the town of Sausalito.

Sausalito. Somewhere beyond it, Gus Klein had followed Judith to a parking lot, where she had entered a bar and disappeared. For about twenty minutes, Klein had said. What was its name? It began with a Z. Ziggie's. Right on the water, Klein had said. Why . . . ?

I almost ran the car off the road. How stupid could a man be? The poem! Death and the sea. Only the day before, Judith had stopped beside the sea and, for a time, mysteriously vanished. Any damned fool should have known instantly that it must be here, somewhere near Ziggie's, that Standish had suggested they meet. Perhaps even in some dark corner of Ziggie's itself. Surely Klein had realized that, immediately after I gave him my interpretation of the poem's final four lines. He would not, of course, trust that conclusion to the point of going directly to Ziggie's and waiting. No, he would follow Judith there.

In the light from the instrument panel I looked at my

wristwatch. It was just past four-thirty. The rendezvous was set for five. I knew without debating it that I would not go directly home. I would stop at Ziggie's. And wait.

Sausalito's main street was thronged with walking shapes that appeared ghostlike in the phosphorescent neon lights mingling with the fog. I crept through the town in second gear. In a few minutes I left the shopping area behind and drove past long, low industrial buildings and marine sales showrooms. I began to think I had overshot my destination when out of the fog, hanging above the road, loomed a sign announcing in red neon script, "Ziggie's." I eased into the driveway and braked to stop but kept the motor running.

From the colored lights fringing the eaves, I could see that it was a low, square, nondescript building set partly on land, partly over the water. Despite the cover of the fog, I decided it would be safer to park elsewhere. I drove through the parking area, exited and drove back a short distance on the opposite side of the main road. A side street suddenly appeared and I made the turn, ran up about twenty yards and parked between the driveways of two frame houses.

It was five minutes to five when I arrived back at Ziggie's on foot. I entered the parking area by way of the exit and worked my way behind a row of cars, parked facing the building, until I came to the entrance driveway. I crossed it quickly, going to another row of parked cars, where I concealed myself behind a dark sedan. The neon sign and an overhead street light provided good visibility. I crouched low, tensing against the chill.

A battered jalopy, psychedelically painted, rattled in carrying teenagers. They parked near the entrance and went noisily inside. Another car, equally dilapidated and with similar passengers, came clattering in next. I began to doubt that this was the meeting place; the clientele was hardly the type Judith would tolerate. A glance at my watch seemed to confirm my error. It was five minutes after five.

Then I saw Judith. She was on foot. Her black-gloved hands clutched a purse, and she was dressed in a gray skirt and a dark, long-sleeved sweater. From her striding walk, I could tell she was wearing flat shoes. She, too, must have parked her car somewhere down the street to escape detection. I pasted myself against the sedan, feeling the cold, wet metal against my cheek, and watched as Judith hurried into the bar.

I waited, anticipating the arrival of Gus Klein, either by car or on foot. Two minutes ticked away. No Klein. Perhaps he had seen her park her car and, knowing her destination, had slipped into the bar ahead of her. I wondered if I could get a glimpse inside without exposing myself.

Striving for nonchalance, I strolled to the near corner of the building and sidled up to the entrance. The top half of the door was clear glass and, peering in, I had a fair view of the smoky interior. There was a small vestibule, then a section of crowded cocktail tables, and beyond that an oval bar next to a miniature dance floor packed with bodies swaying to music from a garishly-lit juke box. The bar was three deep with gesticulating drinkers. If Judith was there, she was not visible.

Disappointed, I stepped back and moved into the shadow of the overhang on the side of the building. I stood on a narrow gravelled path next to a broad strip of blacktop paving running down to the water. A sign told me it was a boat launching ramp for public use. I ran my eyes down its length, wondering what next.

A figure, seeming to emerge from empty space beyond the building, darted onto the ramp near the water line, scurried across and vanished on the other side. It was a woman, unrecognizable, but I knew it had to be Judith; I recalled Gus Klein telling me about the deck and the steps descending to the walkway.

Taking a deep breath, I crossed the ramp and was brought up short by the side of a white clapboard building. Looking up, I saw a scarred sign reading "Marine Supplies—Tackle—Sportfishing." I picked my way along the side and came to a set of wooden stairs attached to the building. Mounting them, I found myself on a narrow deck. From its center a longer flight of stairs led down to a dock. I could hear the water slapping against it, see naked masts bobbing eerily in the undulating whiteness. Was that where Judith had gone? I shuffled down the stairs half way and stopped. If the meeting was being held on one of those anchored boats, I might as well give up. There must have been fifty of them riding the choppy waters. I went back to the deck and moved ahead to the other side. Here, again, there was a short flight of stairs. I jogged down and at the bottom almost slid on my face in mud.

Righting myself, I looked ahead, able to see perhaps twenty yards. I was on a dirt road that ran through what appeared to be a marina shantytown of abandoned boats (many with lights flickering inside), rotting masts and timbers, rusted keels and oil drums. I moved forward out of the mud to the high, rocky crown of the road, past huge, stagnant puddles formed by seepage from the Bay. I heard the muffled sound of sawing and, peering off to the right, saw two long-haired, bearded youths, wearing necklaces of beads, wielding saws. They stopped and looked up, smiling and nodding as I passed. It was obvious I was in the midst of some sort of maritime village of hippie squatters.

The jungle of improvised boat homes thinned out as I proceeded down the road. With each step I felt more lost, more convinced that I had taken the wrong course. Perhaps I should turn back to the marine supply store and hide next to the deck above the berthed boats. Then, if Judith was down there, I could at least see her emerge. But by then she would have concluded her grisly business with Standish and left, so what was the purpose? I slogged dejectedly along, passing a graveyard of beached derelicts too ramshackle for habitation.

I stood for a minute arguing with myself to return to my car and go home. I lost, and continued on. Then, abruptly, there was no place farther to go. Facing me through the fog was a mountain of stinking debris—garbage and dirt and rocks and crates and the roofs of crushed shacks, all intermingled as in some noisome compost heap.

Walking closer, I saw it was piled-up fill for a causeway that already extended into the backwaters of the Bay. Some enterprising but esthetically indifferent individuals were building a marina on the cheap. A short distance from land I could make out the fuzzy silhouette of a huge derrick mounted on a barge, its purpose apparently to deepen the channel.

Suddenly, behind me, a stifled scream pierced the murk. I spun around. About thirty yards back from where I had come, an almost indiscernible figure dashed across the road. Without stopping to think, I broke into a run, shouting, "Wait! Wait!" But the figure only increased its speed, splashing through a mud puddle and disappearing as the scream broke into a long, whimpering sob. Pursuing the sound, I came upon a narrow road forking off in the direction of the highway. I stopped. Further pursuit was useless in that fog. I had no idea who the figure could be. Only that it was a woman and that it was not Judith. The manner of running—knees together, feet splayed—told me the sex. The style of movement, coupled with the tone of the pained outburst, indicated it was someone other than my wife.

I turned toward the Bay, trying to fathom where the woman had come from. Ahead of me was the huge hulk of a vessel, its prow buried deep in the sandy mud. Incredible that the woman could have come from there. Yet, considering the way the hippie squatters lived, it seemed a possibility. If she belonged to that world, her screaming trip might have been one of those bad ones caused by LSD.

I now stood within a few feet of the beached vessel, its prow towering over me. The wooden hull was bleached a light gray, and pocked with holes, exposing rotting ribs. One jagged hole, extending to the ground, was the size of a door. I went inside.

Some light filtered through the broken hull, revealing a slanting, wedge-shaped compartment perhaps fifteen feet across at the widest side and half again as long. The bow section was hidden by a shambles of splintered timbers, rusted oil drums, stiffened coils of frayed rope, canvas tarps green with mold. Apparently none of it was thought worth salvaging. I assumed that the whole dead hulk and its contents would end up as part of the causeway.

I was about to leave, driven out by the stench of dead sea creatures mixed with oil, when I became aware of the steady drip of water. It came from the bow and sounded like rain gurgling down a metal spout.

Curious, I pushed aside some timbers and edged into a small open area, darker than the rest. The sound of running water became louder, coming from somewhere off to the left. I turned my head, blinking to adjust my eyes to the semi-darkness. I was surprised to see a pile of clothing hanging over a shattered spar. I stepped over and reached out.

My hand snapped back as though I had touched a hot stove. It was not a pile of clothing I saw. It was a man, doubled over the spar. The sound was not water. It was blood pouring down on an ancient oil drum.

Something like an angry boil started to form and throb inside my head, something that threatened to burst as, frozen with horror, I listened to the blood gushing on the metal.

I gave my whole body a shake, reached out and grasped the shoulders of the jackknifed body. I turned it over and nearly dropped it.

Plunged into the lower throat between the collarbones was a rusted spike about half an inch in diameter. The mouth gaped. The eyes stared as though seeing a ghost. But the gray eyes of Gus Klein were now forever sightless.

17

The thing inside my head swelled and burst, releasing a vortex of iridescent light. Inside its whirling center I saw myself spinning and falling, crashing through a shower of glass, smashing face down on a warm, ridged surface. Then the sound came gushing out from memory—a deluge of blood pouring from my crushed face onto the accordioned metal of the car's hood. And then the panicked inner shouting, muffled to bestial grunts by a throat that could no longer function:

Judith Judith good God help me! I'm going to die here Judith! Going to die! Where are you Judith? I can't move! I'm trapped in here! Judith sweet heavenly Christ get me out! You've got to get me out! You did it! You Judith! Oh my God my face is gone! I'm dying Judith! And you did it! You Judith! You Judas Judas Judas!

I was outside the boat, bent over and coughing vomit, as the terror slowly subsided. I took out a handkerchief and wiped the spittle from my mouth, the sweat from my forehead. Then I stood straight and stared up at the white ceiling of fog, feeling as if I had experienced divine revelation. But there was no time to ponder it. I rushed back inside the boat.

I had dropped Gus Klein's body back as I had found it. The blood still dripped, but slower now. I found his gray felt hat, spattered red, lying in a puddle of mud on the other side of the oil drum. Dazedly I thought of the all-over grayness of the man and of his gray life. There was nothing I could do for him. Nothing except to help catch the vicious animals who had so brutally skewered out his life. Standish may have wielded the weapon but Judith was just as guilty.

I had to get to a phone and call the police—Bogano, if he could be reached. As if in answer, the wail of sirens started up from somewhere far off. An accident on the highway, I thought.

But it was no accident. It was murder, the murder of Gus Klein to which the sirens were responding. As I lurched out of the boat, I could see, as if through gauze, the headlights of cars swing in from the highway down the road where I guessed the screaming woman had fled. Had she alerted the police? It seemed likely. Her hysterical flight must have resulted from her stumbling upon the body of Gus Klein. Stumbling upon? Why had she been there?

The lead car caught me in its headlights as I ran forward. It pulled up off to the left. A second car, lights in the back window flashing red and yellow, stopped dead in front of me, holding me in its twin beams as an ambulance shrieked to a stop beside it. A huge figure got out of the first car—unmarked, I could now see—and lumbered toward me, hand gripping the handle of a holstered gun. It was Sheriff Bogano. He was followed by his passenger, a square-set man in khakis. Into the bright headlights of the car facing me stepped a man in the dark green uniform of the Highway Patrol. His drawn pistol was aimed straight at my chest. I froze and he lowered it.

Bogano's face was impassive as he came up to me, but his soft voice was edged with disbelief. "Marriott! What are you doing out here?"

I flapped an arm toward the hulk. "Klein," I said. "Gus Klein. He's in there. And he's dead."

That shook Bogano. His chin jutted out from its cushion of sallow flesh. "Klein! Oh, no, they couldn't sucker Klein that way."

I just shook my head and waved a hand for him to go in. He did, accompanied by his partner—a deputy, I thought. When Bogano came out his shoulders were slumped and he moved with labored steps. He tramped over to his car, got in, and I heard him talking in a low voice on the short wave radio.

He came back and asked me again what I was doing out here. I told him. He didn't say it, didn't even look it, but I knew he thought I was a damned fool.

"A woman called in not ten minutes ago," he said. "She was all broken up. Wouldn't give us her name. Just kept saying there was a dead man out here in one of these busted-up boats. I was parked down that road, near the highway, when I got the word on the radio. I came out expecting maybe to find this guy Standish. Surely not Gus Klein. I was standing by in case he needed some help." He glanced balefully at the boat. "He needed it."

I told him about the screaming woman, that I was sure it was not Judith.

"No, she wouldn't be calling the police. Could be someone just happened to wander in. Sounds like she scared off your wife and Standish before they could hide the body. That's what they'd done if they'd had the time. Bad luck for them that woman came by. Good luck for you."

"For me?"

"Yes, if that woman hadn't come screaming out of there, those two wouldn't have taken off. They might have gotten you, too."

I wondered: Could Judith and Standish somehow have set it up to lure *me* to that abandoned boat? It seemed preposterous but . . .

"You think you could identify the woman if you saw her again?"

"No. I only got a quick glimpse of her. I don't think she knew I was even there. She might have come from the hippie colony down the road."

"That might be. We'll check it out. But those people, they don't like to give out much to the fuzz." He said the word sadly.

Those people, attracted by the sirens and the lights, had already begun to gather around. By the time another police car drove in, there were a couple of dozen of them— Christlike men and Godiva haired girls, standing barefoot, like atavistic apparitions, in the swirling fog beyond the lights of the cars. They watched expressionlessly as four men, carrying box-shaped gear, hopped out of the last car and marched into the boat. Through the gaps in the hull I could see the flashing of cameras and hear the sound of feet groaning over timbers.

In about fifteen minutes, a thin little man carrying a black satchel came out and picked his way to where Bogano and I stood in the headlights.

"You can take it away now, Sheriff. They're just finishing up with the prints."

I assumed he was the coroner. Bogano lifted off his hat and flourished it in a signal and the two ambulance men went inside carrying a folded stretcher. When they came out, Gus Klein was on the stretcher covered with a gray blanket. God, I thought, he'll probably be buried in a gray casket. The thought put a lump in my throat.

Bogano and his partner were over talking to the hippies. None of them spoke, replying to questions with a shake of the head, a shrug, a gesture. I had the impression they were less concerned with the murder than with the threat of being forced from their homes.

Coming back, Bogano said, "We'll get no place with them. Unless that woman comes forward, we may have to write her off. Unless she left fingerprints. I'll hope for that, but she may not have been in there long enough to touch a thing."

I thought of something: "I doubt if you'll find any prints from my wife, Sheriff. She was wearing black gloves."

Bogano pushed back his hat and scratched at his dense hairline. "Now that may make things difficult.

Maybe we can get a cast of a shoe print. But my guess is no. Except for the mud puddles, that ground in there's hard as rock."

I had a sinking feeling. "In that case, are you saying we'd have nothing to hold my wife on?"

"Well, there's the telegram Standish sent her. And the photocopy of the letter she sent him. And his taped phone call yesterday. But figure it out. His telegram asked her if she'd meet him—nothing illegal about that. Her answering letter said she would, and suggested The Mountain House—again, no law broken. His call yesterday asked her to look up some poetry, and we decided it meant she should meet him someplace down here—still nothing criminal. Sure, it said something about death, but hell, that could be interpreted any which way. On the face of it, it looks like she just wants to shack up with Standish. Well, alright. We find a dead private eye in that wrecked boat, but supposing we don't find a damn thing that puts her directly on the scene? Mr. Marriott, the D.A. wouldn't touch it. What's more, she may have fixed up some kind of alibi. No, the only one'd know what really happened would be Gus Klein. And you can't put a corpse on the stand."

"Sheriff, is there any question in *your* mind about who killed Gus Klein?"

"The only question is which one used the weapon, Standish or your wife. Likely it was Standish. I've been thinking about it and I think it went something like this. Gus followed your wife to Ziggie's. He knew she'd disappeared going through there before, so this time he waited by the launching ramp, probably behind the corner of the boat and tackle store next door. He saw her come out of Ziggie's back entrance and cross over to the deck of the boat store. He went around front and spotted her on the dirt road. He kept her in sight until she went into that beat-up boat to meet Standish. Standish and your wife must have heard Gus—maybe he tripped over something—and they ducked out of sight. Gus decided to have a look inside. Standish probably had a gun but he didn't want to use it—too many people around. So he—or she—picked up one of those rusty spikes—there're a number of them lying around—and as Gus was nosing around up forward—well, that was it. I'm pretty sure neither of 'em had seen Gus before, so they probably didn't know who it was they killed. The position he was in, I don't think they went inside his coat pockets for identification." Bogano paused and lowered one eyelid. "It's possible when they heard the noise outside, they expected somebody else."

"Any idea who?"

"You. I don't know why they'd think it was you except that your wife maybe figured you'd been tailing her. In that case, why not just murder you right there and get it over with. Then they could bury you someplace in this junkyard and make up some story about you running off. With your amnesia, your wife might just get away with it, at least until she got your money and breezed out of the country. Now, if they'd actually expected Klein, they might have simply sapped him and left him unconscious. You they wanted dead."

A short, compactly built man carrying a square case hopped out of the boat and approached Bogano.

"We lifted two good prints at least. The others are blurred, probably useless. There were none on the spike. Maybe there were at first. But all that blood pourin' down would wash 'em away. Or the killer could've wore gloves. Footprints, forget 'em. Nothin' there worth taking."

An unintelligible voice, sounding like it was frying on a griddle, crackled from Bogano's car. He loped over and slid heavily into the front seat. He said a few words and came back.

"When I got here, I radioed to have a man shot up to your house. Your wife was there when he arrived. Course, she'd have had just about enough time to make it after the killing. But there's something funny. Our man snuck into the garage and got a look at her car. Not a trace of mud or wet on the tires. That wouldn't be the case if she'd driven that car anywhere around Sausalito. Maybe she took a cab. I'll look into it." He gave me an appraising look. "Mr. Marriott, you think you can go home and face your wife like this thing never happened?"

The idea of facing Judith was appalling. "You mean you're not even going to question her?"

"Not yet. I'm not ready to tell her about those bugged messages. And if I don't tell her that, I've got no explanation why I'm dragging her into it. Besides, I want to check out those fingerprints first. If Standish's are among them, which they should be, that may take a bit. We'd have to have 'em matched back East."

I shivered. Miserably I said, "All right. I guess there's nothing to do but face her."

"We'll be nearby if you need us. But I think you'll be safe. I think she's had enough of murder for one night."

"That's comforting."

Bogano looked thoughtful. "It would be good, though, if you could sleep in a separate room."

"I've been doing that. And tonight I'll keep it locked."

18

I was surprised to find myself arriving home only slightly later than usual. Judith's T-Bird was parked in the garage and I examined the tires, confirming what Bogano had been told: they were dry and free of mud. I paced nervously up the short walk to the front door, trying to balance my apprehension with the certainty that Judith would be upstairs locked in her room.

She was not in her room. As I opened the door, I had an oblique view of her sitting on the living room sofa reading a newspaper. She had changed from the sweater and skirt to a dark-green suit. Silence seemed to swell through the house as I reached into the closet and hung up my hat. Turning, the silence was broken by the rustle of the newspaper as Judith laid it down on the cocktail table. I went into the room.

This time there was no radiant smile, no vivacious greeting. Judith's face, though carefully made up, was haggard and solemn, her eyes dull. Without expression she looked past me and said in a neutral voice, "Hello, Dan."

I murmured "Hi" and sauntered over to the table to pick up a section of the paper. A glass sat next to it, half filled with either a martini or straight vodka on the rocks. As I grasped the paper, she said, "I'll fix you a drink, if you like."

The offer made me feel strangely unreal, as if I were in a dream acting out some preposterous charade. Apparently she was now willing to start a conversation. It seemed to me that would be the last thing she would want. It made me curious.

"I'll fix it," I said and went into the kitchen.

Standing beside the sink mixing the drink, I had to remind myself forcibly that the woman sitting quietly inside was a conspirator in murder. The sound of Gus Klein's blood beating down on an oil drum repeated itself in my mind. The picture that had been evoked—of being stretched helplessly on the crumpled, engine-heated hood in a frame of crazed glass as my consciousness bled away—was true. I *knew* it was true. As true as the words I heard: *I'm dying, Judith. And you did it! You Judith! You Judas Judas Judas!* (Was it the herald of total recall?)

I brought my drink into the living room. Picking up the main news section, I sat in a lounge chair off at an angle from her.

"Where have you been all afternoon?" I said casually, opening the newspaper.

"Been?" I caught a startled look. "I've been here at home."

Her voice sounded so sincere that for an instant I almost thought I had imagined her swift entrance into Ziggie's, her furtive exit. So her alibi was to be as simple as that—she had not left the house. Perhaps it would prove unshakable: the car evidently had not left the garage and Bogano had not then had her under surveillance—a dead man had. I stared unseeingly at the paper.

In a monotone, she said, "Dan, I've decided to leave you."

The paper dropped from my hands.

"I've packed two suitcases. They're upstairs. I'm going in a few minutes. I'm taking my car."

She spoke with the indifference of an actress droning through the first reading of a new play. Was she leaving to be rid of me or to escape an inquisition by the police? If it was for the latter reason, it seemed likely she would already have gone, perhaps leaving a cryptic note.

I probed for which reason it was. "Is it because of anything besides"—I hesitated—"besides our recent coolness?"

Her lip curled slightly. "Coolness. *That's* an understatement." She was thinking, I knew, of the night before when she had nakedly thrown herself at me only to be insultingly rebuffed. Her face tightened as she struggled for self-control. "Yes, it is the *coolness*. But, more important, it's the *reason* for the coolness." She hesitated. "For the past week, I've had the feeling of being watched, even followed."

I was surprised but realized she was simply trying to learn how much I knew. Cautiously I said, "What made you think that?"

She looked away. "It was . . . as I said . . . just a feeling."

Perhaps if I shocked her she would betray herself. I spoke bluntly: "The man following you was a detective named Gus Klein."

No recognition showed in her face; it remained impassive. But I saw her hands curl into fists. I waited for some incriminating reply. She said nothing.

"I was the one—not Nancy Mercer—who called the number for the detective agency. It was my first day back at work. I talked to Gus Klein and found out he was the one I had hired to follow you just before the accident."

Even though she did not respond, I felt no regret at telling her. Gus Klein was dead. She was leaving me and would soon know everything, either from the police or when I filed for divorce.

I said, "So, of course, I know about the pictures. I saw the film."

Her voice sighed: "I had hoped your detective might have spared me that, perhaps even have destroyed the negatives after he knew we were back together."

"I had the negatives, not Gus Klein. Four strips of film. I found them the day after we got home, buried in the tobacco humidor in the locked room."

She closed her eyes. "So that's where they were. I should have guessed." She hurried on, as if to avoid explaining the second remark. "I searched everywhere but I never thought of the humidor."

"But you saw the pictures, the prints?"

"My face was practically ground into them. But I got those. They were in your wallet. I burned them over there in the fireplace."

Despite the shock of Gus Klein's death, I was beginning to feel some relief. At least we were getting things out in the open.

"Did you know the . . . the man?" Judith said.

"Yes. Gus Klein told me his name. Ridge Standish."

Judith gave me a searching look. "And I guess you thought I was seeing him again."

I felt the need for evasion. "I didn't know."

"I wasn't, but he did try to contact me. In fact, he left a message with Mirabelle asking me to meet him late this afternoon. I ignored it and stayed home."

The motive behind her frankness was only too clear. She was unaware that I had seen her in Sausalito, confident there was no evidence she had left the house. Therefore she believed she could make it appear that Standish had acted alone to murder Gus Klein, without her presence or knowledge.

I lit a cigarette, not answering.

"Where are the film strips now?" Judith said.

"Sorry, I can't tell you. But they're in a safe place." Safe was the word. They were locked in a big, black quarter-ton of steel in the corner of Klein's office.

"I've tried, without mentioning them," she said, "to explain those pictures. I was a bitter, foolish woman and I've despised myself ever since. But I can't expect you to understand—you have no memory of the way we were."

I resisted answering. Once more—through the employment of limited honesty garnished with humility—she was trying to present herself in a sympathetic light.

She slid to the edge of the sofa and finished her drink. "Well, you have all the evidence you need for a divorce. But you won't need it, not the pictures. I won't contest it. You can divorce me anywhere and on any basis you choose."

Again she had surprised me. "Divorce," I said as though seriously considering it for the first time. "Yes, perhaps that's the only answer." I paused. "Of course, we'll have to decide on some sort of settlement."

"I'll leave that entirely to you. You've always been more than fair, Dan."

Now it was all utterly clear. She was throwing herself on my mercy in the hope of inflating my generosity. If, as she supposed, I had not heard from Ginnie about her past lubricity, had not suspected her of trying to kill me, had not practically witnessed her part in Klein's murder, I would lean over backwards to be liberal, perhaps even destroy the film strips. That was what she was now angling for, using her admissions as bait. If she succeeded, she would have enough money for a reasonably comfortable life with Ridge Standish, provided both could escape the consequences of killing Gus Klein. She was taking a last, hopeful chance. But, unless she was prepared to add to her conscience the burden of a second corpse—me—and apparently she was not—it was the only chance she had left.

"I'll think about the settlement," I said. "Where do you plan to go?"

"I don't know exactly. I'll just drive down the coast and stop someplace for a few days at first. When I get a bit settled, I'll let you know where I am. Will you hold up filing the divorce until then?"

"Yes." She was going, I knew, to Standish. The thought made me uneasy. But I dismissed it from my mind. Bogano's men would be following, prepared to arrest her and her lover as soon as they met. At last, thank God, I would be out of it.

"I'm going now," she said. She stood up and looked at me strangely for a moment. Then her whole body began to shake violently and she darted for the stairs.

I waited until I heard the bathroom door slam, then followed her to pick up the luggage. As I walked into the bedroom, I heard her in the bathroom getting sick.

Each of the beds sagged under a large suitcase, lids closed, clasps fastened. On impulse, I went to the nearest one, quietly opened the clasps and lifted the lid. The clothes obviously had been flung in heedlessly. I worked my hands around and came upon a gray skirt wrapped in a black, long-sleeved sweater—the outfit, I was sure, Judith had worn earlier. The sound of the toilet flushing jerked me upright. Then I heard the water running in the wash basin and bent again to the suitcase. My hand slid down the side and touched a balled-up article that had a familiar buttery feel. I took it out. Leather gloves. The tight-fitting kind Judith always wore into town.

I inspected the first one that came to hand. Nothing. It was the left glove. I smoothed out the other and looked closely at the palm. In the center was a small spot of some nondescript color. It could have been put there by any number of things, including perhaps a rusted spike.

I heard the bathroom doorknob turn and quickly pushed the gloves into the suitcase. Judith did not come out at once—she had probably forgotten something. When she did, tucking a toothbrush into her purse, I was on my way with the bags.

After I loaded them into the trunk of the T-Bird, we merely nodded goodbye and Judith drove off. I followed her down the driveway and in less than five seconds a black sedan with two men in it pulled up next to me. They identified themselves as homicide inspectors and asked my wife's destination. When they found I didn't know, they roared off. I had no time to tell them about the gloves.

Back in the kitchen making another drink, the reaction finally set in. My hands trembled and a visceral quaking danced me from one foot to the other. I managed to down a straight vodka and then another. Almost immediately I felt a physical calmness. I made a long vodka tonic and took it into the living room. Slumped in a chair, I stared vaguely at the depressions left by Judith in the sofa cushions. Without thinking, I got up and toured the house, locking all the doors.

The result was a feeling of entombment. I paced the floor, made another drink, smoked incessantly, started to prepare some food then gave it up. I brought a drink into the living room and sat morosely in front of the television set observing a mustached young man briskly reviewing the events of the day. It was almost seven-fifteen and the news was going off.

"Locally," the man said, "the body of a man, his throat impaled by a spike, was found late this afternoon in a battered and abandoned boat just north of Sausalito. The man was identified as Gus Klein, owner and operator of a private detective agency in San Francisco. Police are investigating. Next, a report on the weather, after this message."

That did it. I flipped off the TV. I had to get out of this house, talk to someone, anyone. There was but a single choice—Jeb Scott. That meant seeing Ginnie, but I refused to worry about that.

Jeb's voice came choking through the phone like that of a man in pain. "I'm glad you called, Dan. Something is wrong with Ginnie. I've never seen her like this before."

Abstractedly I asked if it was flu, there was a lot of it around.

"God no, not flu. When I got home, I found her in her room sobbing hysterically. Her eyes had a wild look to them. She wouldn't talk to me, wouldn't communicate at all. Just sat on the edge of the bed sobbing uncontrollably." He breathed heavily. "Like she'd suddenly seen a dead man."

In the grisly context of the last two hours, the words exploded in my ear with horrifying significance. It was a moment before I could dismiss the remark for what I was sure it was—a meaningless cliche.

"You must be damned upset, Jeb. Is there anything I can do?"

"No, the doctor was here. Said it looked like a typical case of shock. Gave her a big hypo of something and left, about half an hour ago. Ginnie's sleeping now. Oh. What were you calling about?"

"Nothing really, Jeb. I was thinking about stopping by. But certainly not now, unless there's some way I can help."

"Damned right you can help, just by you and Judith coming over. I've got the jitters sitting here alone."

"I'm afraid Judith isn't available. But if you like, I'll come."

"I'd appreciate that, Dan."

When I arrived, Jeb was in the library pouring out brandy. Though I hadn't eaten, I accepted one and we sat in the two chairs facing each other. Jeb now appeared in control of himself.

"Damnedest thing about Ginnie," he said. "Thought at first she'd been in some sort of accident. Still think that's a possibility but there's no damage to the car. Even though it *is* a mess."

I asked what was wrong with it.

"Splattered with mud, as though she'd been running it through puddles. Now, there shouldn't be any mud puddles around here; thank God we're out beyond the damned summer fog. You could *cut* it on the Bridge tonight—thick and wet. Ginnie might have been in that area, perhaps Sausalito, shopping. Even so, I don't see how she could pick up all that muck on the road."

The hair on the back of my neck bristled.

"Even mud on her shoes and stockings."

Could it be that the woman who had screamed and fled was Ginnie Scott? It seemed an insane idea, yet, to my knowledge, she was the only person besides Bogano who knew Gus Klein was checking on Judith. I had told her about it shortly before Klein tapped our phone. What reason would Ginnie have for following Judith, assuming she had? Was it to prove that Judith's passion for Standish still flourished? Did she thus hope to incite me into divorcing Judith immediately and marrying her? If so, why was Ginnie's attitude toward me so deliberately distant? I was baffled. One thing, however, was apparent: If Ginnie had stumbled upon that bleeding, lifeless body of Gus Klein, no doctor was needed to diagnose the cause of her present symptoms.

". . . but enough of that," Jeb was saying. "We'll hear all about it when she comes around. The doctor didn't seem particularly worried." He sipped his brandy. "Now about you. Did Judith forsake you for some of her club-women tonight?"

My depression plus the drinks made me decide to tell him, up to a point. "Judith and I have separated. She left shortly before I came over here."

Jeb's eyebrows rose. "You mean a spat. Nothing serious?"

"Yes, serious. We've agreed to divorce."

Jeb set his glass down slowly. He drew a silk handkerchief from his top pocket and patted his lips. "Dan, I hope that nothing that I told you led to this decision. I said it before and I'll say it again, Judith had once indulged in a few harmless flirtations. Nothing more, I'm sure."

He understood my wife no better than he did his own. But his obtuseness made me feel no less shame at having cuckolded him, a man who had trusted me as a partner and a friend. "No," I said, "it's a lot deeper than that. I can't explain but there's just no chance of our making it. I don't like to inflict it on you but I thought you'd better hear it from me instead of someone else."

Jeb lit a cigar and contemplated the tip. He made a wry face. "This isn't our night, Dan. First, Ginnie comes home out of her mind, and now you tell me you and Judith are getting a divorce. I suggest . . ."

"Yes! Divorce her! Divorce her! Now!"

I whirled in my chair. It was Ginnie, wearing only a nightgown, clutching to the frame of the open door.

"Ginnie!" Jeb had sprung half way across the room. She stopped him with: *"Murder! That's what she did! Murder!"*

I was standing. Jeb looked at me in bewilderment.

Ginnie flung out an arm toward me. "Murder! That's all she knows! Murder!" Her eyes were glazed with delirium. She looked and sounded like some creature in a nightmare; which, to herself, reliving the traumatic experience, her mind warped by the drug, she probably was.

Jeb was at her side. She looked at him vapidly for a moment, gave a strangled cry, and collapsed into his arms.

19

Sheriff Bogano called me the next morning while I was having coffee.

"Those fingerprints we lifted—we checked them out. Too bad most of them weren't much more than smears."

Alarmed, I said, "But your man said there were two good prints."

"That's right. Neither of them your wife's. I expected that—you said she was wearing gloves. The two good prints are Standish's. We sent them back to Washington last night and they match the ones on his service record. He fought in Korea."

I breathed easier. At least they had decisive evidence against one of the murderers.

"I'd say some of the others have got to belong to that woman you saw running away."

Ginnie. I couldn't drag her into it, at least not until she had recovered. I had done enough to hurt her, and Jeb as well. He had appeared shaken and confused, for the first time registering self-doubt. Perhaps he was finally realizing that his wife was truly human.

Bogano said, "Now, something more important. I phoned you last night but got no answer. I'd have tried again but after what you'd been through, I decided you needed sleep. What I want to ask—why did your wife take off for God-knows-where right after you got home?"

I briefed him on my talk with Judith. "She told me I could divorce her. No contest. She seems to think I'll give her a fair settlement."

"Well, I'm going on the belief you'll never have to pay out. If it's the last thing I do, I'm going to get her charged with the murder of Gus Klein and convicted of the murder of Gus Klein." Bogano's voice vibrated with zealous intensity. "And the same goes for Ridge Standish."

I had been wanting to tell him about the black gloves and the suspicious spot. Now I did.

"You kept them?"

"I didn't have a chance. She was coming out of the bathroom."

Bogano made a clucking noise. "Too bad. We could have made a chemical analysis of the spot. Well, she'd have gotten rid of those gloves by now. So we still don't have a damned thing on her."

Had he learned anything about how Judith had been transported to the boat?

"That's a blank, too. We checked out every taxi company in the county. None of them had sent a cab to your address. Sure, she could have hiked to town and caught a cab at a stand. But not one Kentwood cab dropped a passenger off in Sausalito yesterday afternoon."

"How about a bus?"

"Of course, that could be. But, Mr. Marriott, if a woman was going someplace to meet her lover, maybe plan a murder, I just don't think she'd take a bus."

Particularly Judith, I thought. "Do you know where my wife is now?"

"I do. I talked to one of our men last night and again about twenty minutes ago. She stopped at a motel in Paso Robles. That's about half way to L.A. She checked in for only one night, so maybe she's already on her way south again. How far she'll go, I wouldn't know. I'm just hoping she'll meet up with Standish. On him, we got out an APB, alerted the border guards and asked cooperation from the Mexican police. Nothing to report. He's as slippery as they come."

Suddenly I remembered something and almost dropped the phone. As far as I knew, Gus Klein had never told the sheriff that Standish was wanted for embezzlement. Now, apologetically, I reported everything I knew, explaining that Klein's silence was based on the fear that a massive manhunt would only alert Standish just when Klein thought he had him trapped.

Bogano grunted in surprise. "I'll be damned." He was silent a moment. "Poor old Gus. One mistake and it cost him his life."

He started to ring off. Then: "Oh, one other thing. We're keeping Klein's bug on your phone. In this business, you never know."

The thought of the bug was disconcerting but I offered no objection.

I left for work later than usual. As I started out the

door, Mirabelle came in. While she was hanging up her coat, I told her that Judith would be away for a couple of weeks on a trip. Later, there could be another explanation.

I started out, then stopped. "By the way, Mirabelle, when you left yesterday afternoon, was Mrs. Marriott here? I forgot to ask her about something."

"Yessir. She was here."

"What time did you leave?"

"Lessee. Little past four o'clock."

"You're sure she was here?"

"Well, yessir. She drove me down to the bus." She grinned, showing gold teeth. "I 'member thinkin' about maybe I'd have to take a taxi, like sometimes. That's 'cause I didn't see Mrs. Marriott anywhere around and thought she was out. Then I walked out by the pool and saw her way down in the corner fiddlin' around with those boxes of red flowers."

I felt a mild curiosity. During the time I had been home from the hospital I had never seen Judith so much as touch a flower. Everything was cared for by a gardener who came in twice a week.

Mirabelle disappeared into the kitchen. I strolled out to the pool, going to the farthest corner of the flagstone terrace. There, under the shade of live oaks, a chest-high retaining wall supported four long boxes of blooming petunias. I inspected each box, seeing nothing out of the ordinary. Except perhaps for the last box. Lying on top of one plant were a few twigs similar to those in the uncultivated area beyond the wall. Rising to my toes, I looked over. A section of ground about a foot long and half a foot wide appeared to have been disturbed, then covered with dry leaves. Pushing them aside, I explored the dirt with my hands. It seemed less tightly packed than the surrounding earth. I went to the garden shed and came back with a trowel. The earth came up quickly, revealing what amounted to an oblong compartment about eight inches deep walled with hard dirt.

The thought that had been prowling the back of my mind sprang forward: the earthen compartment was an excellent place to cache a gun. Judith had said that long ago she threw the gun into the Bay. I was certain she had lied, that she had dug it up and taken it with her. Perhaps for protection, perhaps to prevent its being found, or both.

I pushed back the dirt and the leaves. It was no concern of mine now. But I called Bogano. He seemed more interested in Judith's hiding of the weapon than in her personal possession of it. But he said, "Okay, I'll tell our men she's armed."

When I got to the office, Jeb had not arrived. It was nine-thirty. I waited until ten before calling to ask how Ginnie was feeling.

His voice was weary. "She's in County Hospital. Took her there about an hour ago. Just got back. Dan, I'm frightened. She just stares. Almost catatonic. And mumbles. Still that nonsense about murder. She acts like I'm with her but somehow I'm not."

I restrained myself from blurting out the story of Gus Klein. The fatal stabbing would only raise more questions in his mind than it answered: What was Ginnie doing in that old hulk? Who was Gus Klein? A detective? Was he following someone? Who? Could Ginnie have been involved? Etcetera. The answers, however euphemized, would only unnerve him further.

". . . under sedation. Doctors are still treating her for shock. I won't be in but I'll keep you posted."

Jeb called in after lunch. "Just checking with my secretary and thought I'd let you know—Ginnie seems to be coming around. She's exhausted, of course, and hardly talks at all, but she's conscious and rational."

"Did she say what caused all this?"

"No, and right now she doesn't seem to want to say. Naturally, I'm not pushing her."

"Is she allowed visitors?"

"I'd say not yet, Dan. You might call her this evening. There's a phone by the bed."

I spent a good deal of the afternoon looking at my watch and at the phone. Every minute I expected Bogano to call with the news that Judith had been apprehended with Standish. If she had left Paso Robles early in the morning, she would have had time to cross the Mexican border. The phone remained mute. By four o'clock I was so tense that I went downstairs to the bar and had a drink. When I returned, Nancy Mercer handed me a phone message. Sheriff Bogano, please call back. I felt as if I had rubbed a lamp instead of a glass of scotch.

Bogano's voice was vibrant with controlled anger. "We lost her. Your wife. She got away."

"How? Where?"

"It was a freak thing. At least I think it was. I doubt

your wife knew she was being followed. She was sailing down the freeway in Los Angeles, our men two cars behind. Both cars were in the fast lane. Then, just before reaching one of the Hollywood off-ramps, your wife suddenly darts through an opening in the traffic, crosses the three inner lanes, and shoots down the ramp. Our men had to tool right past—that traffic's fast and heavy—and they couldn't get off the freeway for another half mile. Now, that L.A.'s one hell of a big city, more like six cities. If she's planning to hole up there, our men might as well go home to their wives. But we've got the L.A. police in on it, and maybe we'll have just a little bit of luck."

I felt more depressed than anxious. "Nothing on Standish, I suppose."

"That's another thing I want to talk to you about." Bogano's voice lowered to a growl. "Mr. Marriott, could you stop by my office on your way home?"

"Yes. I can leave right away. You mean there is some news on Standish?"

"News, yes. But not about where he is. If it checks out, it makes the whole case cockeyed."

"What is it?"

"Wait till you get here. By then I may know if it's true or if somebody goofed. It's about a teletype I got from New York. I'm still trying to figure out how it affects our case against Standish. And I still don't believe it."

20

Sheriff Bogano pushed his sausage-like fingers through black ropes of hair, then shook his head. "This morning, Mr. Marriott, after you told me about the embezzlement, I sent a long teletype to the New York police. It was a complete report on Standish's activities as far as we knew them—the messages picked up on your phone, the letter in San Diego, Standish's fingerprints in the boat, and of course the murder itself. Just before I called you this afternoon, I got a teletype back from them."

Bogano picked up a square piece of yellow paper, stared at it and shook his head again. I started to reach for it but Bogano dropped it to the desk as though unaware of me.

"I'm waiting now for a call from that guy you mentioned—Marshall Whitley—in Greenwich, Connecticut. I called him at four-fifteen—seven-fifteen in Greenwich. A butler answered and said Whitley was due within the hour and would call back. It's now five-thirty—eight-thirty back there—and Whitley hasn't called." Bogano picked up the yellow paper and handed it to me. "Here, it's short. Much too short."

It took me a moment to get past all the identification symbols. Then I read: "Ridge Standish no longer wanted by this department or any other police authorities. Full report being mailed to your office. George Sullivan, Chief of Police, N.Y.C."

My mind blurred as though thrown out of focus. I looked up at Bogano's impassive face, then back to the teletype. I was trying to relate the words to what we knew of Standish, or thought we knew, when the phone rang.

Bogano snatched it from the cradle, snapped, "Yes, Bogano speaking," listened, then nodded at me: Marshall Whitley was coming on.

In a moment Bogano announced his name again, stated his official position, and came directly to the point. "Mr. Whitley, I've got a teletype here from the New York Chief of Police. I'll read it to you." He read it slowly, enunciating distinctly. "Is this true?" A pause. "I'd appreciate an explanation, Mr. Whitley."

Bogano listened for a long while, occasionally punctuating the silence with a brief question. When he hung up, he examined his torn green desk blotter and tugged at his lower lip. Finally he looked up at me out of clouded eyes.

"Unbelievable," he said. "Unbelievable but true." He gave his head a snap, like a boxer muddled by a punch. "Here's the story. Maybe if we both try real hard, we can make some sense out of it."

Bogano unfastened a shirt button and reflectively scratched his matted chest. "As you know, Standish was a partner in a New York brokerage named Stone and Whitley. Marshall Whitley is president. Stone—August Stone—is executive veepee. Ridge Standish headed up a special department serving only well-heeled customers, men whose investments amounted to a hundred thousand dollars or more. They were charged a service fee as well as commissions. Millions of dollars of stocks and bonds were bought and sold every year by Standish's department. In a great many cases, the securities were turned over to Standish for safekeeping. The only one he reported to—in fact, who handled a lot of the transactions himself—was August Stone, the executive veepee. It was this August Stone, who, Whitley told me, insisted back last November that Standish get away on a long vacation. It made sense because Standish had split with his wife—which probably cost him a bundle—and was feeling very low."

Bogano lit up a thin black cigar and blew two enormous smoke rings. I was already on my second cigarette.

"Well, I guess you see where I'm heading, Mr. Marriott. Standish wasn't the embezzler—August Stone was. He'd got himself way over his head in the market and he needed cash to bail himself out. Over a period of time, he'd been selling securities that weren't his and using the proceeds to stay afloat. Of course, he always expected to re-purchase them with no one the wiser. And for awhile he was able to do just that. Then, as you know, Whitley discovered that a big chunk of their customers' securities was missing. More than three hundred thousand dollars worth. All of them negotiable. He went to August Stone and Stone laid all the blame on Standish. Why not? The securities were Standish's responsibility, he ran the department. And he'd taken off for two months. Whitley says that at first he couldn't bring himself to believe it was Standish. He'd trusted him like a son. And he remembered that Standish had called in to the office several times while he was away. That didn't sound like a guilty man. But the evidence seemed damning, and after Standish didn't show when he was due, in January, Whitley finally whistled for the cops and the story broke wide open."

Bogano contemplated the ash on his cigar. "Well, alright. Then why, if Standish knew he wasn't the embezzler, didn't he rush back and try to prove it? Two reasons, I think. One—and this comes from Whitley—Standish knew what August Stone was up to and was apparently accepting hush money from Stone. Whitley says that the audit showed some forty thousand dollars couldn't be accounted for. That sum, he's sure, was paid by Stone to Standish for keeping his mouth shut. That would explain his calls to the office while he was on that vacation—he was checking in with Stone to find out if everything was okay. There's no way to prove this against Standish— Stone refused to say a word about the missing forty thousand—and Whitley's not going to try. Standish probably knew they weren't going to prosecute him but why go back to New York and test it? Especially when he was out of a job and it was unlikely any other brokerage would hire him. Those things get around fast. So he just stayed in Mexico, except for the week or ten days when he came up here prior to your accident."

Bogano paused and I said, "That explains why Standish used his own name in Mexico and at the Mark Hopkins hotel up here. He felt safe."

"Yes, and it explains something else. Let's say he kept a good part of the forty thousand Stone paid him. And maybe he had some of his own money. Maybe—just guessing—fifty thousand all told. Now it makes a little more sense that he'd be close to broke when he called your wife last week. I can believe that he might have run through most of fifty thousand in less than a year. But three hundred thousand—that was hard to swallow."

"When did they learn August Stone was really the thief?"

"Whitley got the word only a few days ago. Stone had been up to his old tricks but this time went too far. It took Whitley awhile to digest it and face Stone with the report."

"You said there were two reasons why Standish didn't go back. It seems enough that he was being paid off by August Stone and could have been prosecuted. But I guess the second reason was my wife."

"Your wife and you. Standish's own wife had run out on him, so he was pretty well softened up for any woman who thought he was the Great Man. Apparently your wife did. Standish fell for her. And it looks like your wife more than returned the compliment. She'd been on the outs with you, so Klein told me, and that helped make Standish a lot more than just a passing fancy. In fact—and if it wasn't a sure thing before, it is now—your wife was so taken with Standish, she tried to kill you to get him."

"Yes," I said, "and Standish was willing to have her do it. He'd not only get her, he'd also get the money. And you've proved to me that he needed it."

"But when he found out you'd survived the accident, he chickened out. He skipped out of the hotel, not paying, and leaving his luggage. With you alive, Standish could see himself being named corespondent in a messy divorce suit—one your wife couldn't win. And if she couldn't win, there'd've been little or no money. Sure, he also wanted to put a lot of distance between himself and the law. The way it looked, you might have your wife charged with attempted murder and drag him into it."

"But why did he wait for eight months before contacting my wife? Why is he willing to risk everything now when he wasn't before?"

"He might just recently have heard about your amnesia and therefore figured you as no threat. But more important, I think, is his desperate need for money. To the point, the way it looks, where he's willing to settle for a lot less than he'd hoped for. But he wasn't planning to take loser's share. I'm convinced he met your wife in that boat to plot your murder. If successful, they'd have had the jackpot. Then Klein trailed along and that blew it. Gus Klein may have given you some life insurance, Mr. Marriott. Because, sure as hell, they couldn't get rid of you now and make it look like an accident. And I think you can be sure they won't try."

The reassurance was wasted. I still felt nervous. "Where does that leave us now?"

Bogano pulled at his jowls. "Mr. Marriott, I guess all

we've just had was an exercise. We're right back where we were. We still want Standish and your wife for the murder of Gus Klein. The case against Standish should be open and shut—we've got more motive than we need and we've got his fingerprints at the murder scene. Against your wife, we've got motive but nothing else. But if we can catch them together, we should at least be able to sock it to her as an accessory."

I jumped as Bogano's phone rang. He let it ring a second time before absently picking it up. A voice crackled excitedly through the receiver.

"What!" Bogano thrust forward in his chair in an elephantine charge. He listened intently, big eyes standing out on his cheeks like oysters.

"You say there's not much left. How much?"

Bogano's huge body became more taut as the voice rasped on. He eyed me mysteriously over the receiver jammed against his jaw.

"When will you hear from ballistics?"

The answer made Bogano blow out in disgust. "That long. All right. You call me the minute you've got anything. Anything." Bogano slammed down the receiver.

Not looking at me, he dragged his bulk to the window. He turned his back, spread his legs, knotted his hands behind him. I must have waited two minutes and he still had not moved.

Finally I said, "That sounded like bad news."

He turned slowly. His eyes glared like a trapped animal's. He slapped exasperatedly at his gun, as if aching to use it.

"Mr. Marriott," he said, chewing the words, "it looks like we've lost our prime suspect for the murder of Gus Klein."

I was too stunned to speak. One thought seared through my mind: Judith had killed herself.

"Right now the homicide lab is checking out a bullet that I'm sure as I stand here will match that gun your wife dug up. It's registered, so we know the make and caliber."

"You mean Judith . . ."

"I mean your wife pumped a bullet through the heart of Ridge Standish. He's dead. And your wife's still at large, God only knows where!"

21

From Bogano's office I drove down to the main street and stopped at a bar. Sitting on a red stool sipping my first vodka, I couldn't have been more bewildered if I'd had a dozen.

So stunning was Bogano's bitter announcement that I could not think to ask an intelligent question. I could only speculate numbly on Judith's motive for the slaying— presumably the unanticipated murder of Klein and Judith's greatly diminished financial worth had provoked Standish to jilt her once again. Bogano, preoccupied, growled unintelligible comments, finally forcing me to leave by saying he had business to attend to.

Ordering a second drink, I considered the position in which Judith now found herself. This time it appeared that the police had tangible evidence of her guilt—a bullet. Every law officer in every county and village would be on the lookout for her. She probably had only a small amount of cash, and her car, and she would doubtless have to abandon the car. She was alone, with no one to turn to. Unless she could somehow make it across the border, change her identity, perhaps take up with another man, she was a goner.

It was seven-thirty when I drove the Porsche into the garage. Darkness had gathered, only a faint glow appearing over the western ridge of the mountain. I picked up the evening paper on the front walk, let myself in and went to the kitchen and made a tall drink. Snapping on the pool lights, I went outside and stretched out on a divan, seeking the calmness that often came from looking at the clear blue water. Tonight it had no effect. I drank half the drink and went back inside, snapping off the pool lights.

I sat in a lounge chair in the living room and read the front page of the newspaper. It screamed with the story of Gus Klein's murder, showing a picture of Gus as he looked alive, one of his blanketed body as it was slid into the ambulance, another of the deserted boat. Everything that was reported I already knew. As expected, Judith and Ridge Standish were not mentioned. I got nothing from the story except a deep sadness.

Although not at all hungry, I went to the kitchen, heated a can of soup and forced down half of it. Standing at the counter, I was swept by a strange feverishness that seemed to emanate from a buzzing focal point in the back of my head. I tried to throw it off by going outside and walking around the dark pool. Far overhead the blinking lights of a jetliner made me feel like a solitary bug, as lonely as when I first regained consciousness in the hospital. Perhaps that's what made me remember to call Ginnie Scott.

When the phone rang in her room, Jeb answered. For the first time since witnessing Ginnie's traumatic behavior, he sounded relaxed.

"Ginnie's in an examination room. Just some routine nonsense, the doctor says. Nothing at all to worry about. Nothing."

"Good. I'm glad she's back to normal."

"Well, I wouldn't say normal exactly. Still doesn't want even to mention the cause of all this. In fact, she scarcely talks at all. But a little time should take care of that."

Under the circumstances, I could hardly tell Jeb about Judith and Standish, let alone Gus Klein.

With uncharacteristic humility, Jeb said, "I think I've learned something from this, Dan. I always took Ginnie for granted. But not any more."

"I understand, Jeb. If there's anything I can do . . ."

"Thanks, but not a thing, Dan. Ginnie's got plenty to read and there's a TV above the foot of the bed. You might stop by and see her some time tomorrow. That might help." His voice lowered with concern. "Have you heard from Judith?"

It was a relief to say honestly that I had not.

"I'll tell Ginnie you called."

When I rang off, the walls of the house seemed to close in. Looking up, the stairs appeared to form an odd geometric pattern of wavering lines. It was frighteningly like something I had heard about: the warning aura an epileptic experiences prior to a seizure. I rubbed my eyes, swayed into the living room and switched on the television set. I sat down in front of it, my arms resting leadenly on the chair arms, breath coming faster, body limp with sudden exhaustion. As though from a distance, I heard the sound of galloping and gunfire but was oblivious to the picture flashing on the tube. I lit a cigarette but inhaled only once before grinding it out. My heart thumped against my ribs. The air became suffocating.

Was I having a heart attack? I doubted it. I felt no pain in the chest or shoulder; in fact, except for a stiffness in the neck, there was no pain anywhere. Something Dr. Ragensburg had once said came back to me. He had been describing the symptoms of anxiety. I took a deep breath. Based on what he said, I was having an anxiety attack.

"... *body of a man named Ridge Standish. Authoritative police sources state that the identity of the killer is known but that they are not yet ready to make an arrest. This has been a special news bulletin from KRBC-TV.*"

The words jolted like an electric shock. I jerked forward, feeling my eyes dilate in the glare of the picture tube. Nothing that was there indicated the announcer had intervened. The message was lost in the trample of hoofs, the bloodcurdling whoops of attacking Indians. The western had resumed. I got up, switched it off and returned shakily to the chair.

It was after eight o'clock, two hours since I had left Bogano. The bullet extracted from Standish's body had apparently been verified as coming from Judith's gun. Had it been Bogano who notified the press? Doubtful, or his name would probably have been given instead of the vague "authoritative police sources." The story more likely had been broken by some policeman friendly to a reporter.

My thoughts were disturbed by a sound coming from somewhere at the rear of the house. Deer or raccoons, I thought, identifying the metallic sound as the quick displacement of a garbage can lid. It was a common occurrence, I had heard. I lurched to my feet and walked stiffly through the dark kitchen to the back steps. Just as I thought—the lid of the garbage can showed a gap. I fastened the lid tightly and returned to the living room.

The incident had provided a brief distraction from my intense discomfort. But now it struck full force, as if all my senses were conspiring against sanity. I paced the floor, massaging my neck. Strange noises throbbed in my ears, defying recognition as real or imaginary. Could some of them be coming from outside the door? Was it possible that Bogano still had the house under surveillance? In desperation, I seized on the notion. It would be an excuse to talk to Bogano, perhaps even learn that Judith had been caught.

In my haste to dial, I got a wrong number. I tried again and got the sheriff's office but not Bogano. He was out, the man said, and might not be back for some time. Was it important that I reach him? Who was calling? I hung up without leaving my name. Why let the sheriff know I was badgering him?

Sweat suddenly bathed my body. Dizzily I slid down on the small chair next to the telephone table and dropped my head between my knees.

The phone shrieked into my ear. I leaped up, dithered with the receiver, finally got it pressed to my head. It was Ginnie Scott, her voice a hoarse whisper.

"Are you all right?" she said.

I lied that I was.

"Jeb had no sooner left when I heard an announcement on television about Ridge Standish."

"Yes, I heard it too." The sound of a human voice eased my tension. I found myself babbling, "The suspect wasn't mentioned, but it's Judith. She left here last night, right after Gus Klein's body was found. The police followed her to Los Angeles. They lost her there. I stopped to see Sheriff Bogano just before coming home tonight. While I was sitting there, he got the call that Standish had been found shot to death. The police lab was examining the bullet. It looks like they proved it came from the same kind of gun Judith was carrying."

There was silence. I guessed Ginnie was overwhelmed by my outburst.

When she spoke, it was in a small but firm voice. "I started it all." The voice broke slightly. *"I'm* responsible for Gus Klein's murder."

My hand turned clammy on the receiver. "Ginnie, you're upset. You don't know what you're saying."

"I *do* know. That first telephone message that Mirabelle gave Judith from someone named Stanton—that came from a man I hired. A man I got right out of the classified pages. He called again later and got you. He hung up without speaking. That was to get *you* more suspicious."

"Ginnie, why don't you try to get some sleep. I'll stop by tomorrow and we'll talk about it."

She ignored the implication, going on breathlessly. "Right after that—the same day—I called. Judith was out, and you told me Gus Klein was going to tap your phone. That fit in with my plans perfectly. I arranged to have the telegram sent from Ensenada asking Judith to write Standish in San Diego to say if she'd meet him. That telegram was as much a test as anything—to find out if she'd play my little game. The man I hired picked up the letter in San Diego."

I sank down into the chair. It was clear Ginnie was telling the truth.

"The Mountain House was not the place I hoped Judith would suggest for a meeting. She chose it, I think, because it's crowded there. She could conceal herself and make sure the man who arrived was the one she expected. So then I thought of the Shelley poem in Palgrave's. I knew Judith had a copy. I had the message referring to it called in to your house when Judith was out. Mirabelle took it."

Weakly I said, "But why did you suggest—through the poem—that the meeting be held by the sea? Death and the sea is what the last four lines are all about."

"I knew there was something important down by the Bay and I thought I knew what it was. I'd followed Judith before but lost her. So had Gus Klein. I saw him waiting for her outside of Ziggie's. She'd gone there and disappeared for awhile. I followed Judith again yesterday."

Dimly I remembered about Judith's car. "How did Judith get there? Bogano's certain she didn't use her T-Bird."

"Oh, she's cunning. She drove up to the Ford showroom on 101. That's where she'd bought the T-Bird she has. She said she wanted to take out one of the new ones for a demonstration drive. At least, I assume that. I saw the salesman wave goodbye. She wanted to make sure there was no evidence of her own car being down by the Bay should something go wrong. I'm sure she wasn't trying to avoid being followed. She *wanted* to be followed but she didn't think it would be by Gus Klein. Anyway, she drove down to Sausalito, parked down the other side of the main street, and walked back to Ziggie's."

"My God, Ginnie, I saw her go in—and then come out of the back entrance. I'd just come from the office."

The phone was silent a moment.

"I'm not surprised," Ginnie said. "I expected you to figure out the Shelley poem but I thought at least you would stick with Gus Klein." Her voice quavered. "I didn't anticipate what happened next. I waited a couple of minutes until Judith was out of sight on that muddy road. Then I followed along. When I got near the old boat, I heard a dreadful moaning sound. I rushed in. Judith was gone. But"—now she groaned out the words—"but Gus Klein was there. Dead. And all because of this wild plan I had."

My mind was whirling. "Ginnie, what made you think of it?"

"I wanted to scare Judith into giving herself away. She knew that whoever had sent those messages had found out, or guessed, her secret. She was gambling that that person would follow her to the boat alone. Well, she got the wrong one. Gus Klein arrived first. She was hiding inside gripping that spike—it would have been too risky to use a gun. When she heard Klein exploring the front of the boat, she crept up on him. It was dark there and

I'm sure she thought it was someone else. But then she suddenly knew differently. Apparently he turned just as she stabbed at him and the spike plunged into his—" The sentence trailed off in a whimper.

My mind was spinning. "You say she was expecting someone else . . ."

"Yes, the one she *thought* had arranged the phone calls, sent the telegram . . ."

"Ridge Standish," I said impatiently.

She hesitated. "Yes."

"But why would she want to murder him then?"

Ginnie's voice rose piercingly. "Because Standish was through with her! Because Standish, *being* through with her, would most likely turn her over to the police when and if he finally remembered!"

"Remembered? What in God's name are you talking about?"

Savagely she snapped back, "Didn't you ever suspect? That wasn't Ridge Standish's body the police dug up in that old boat. It was Dan Marriott—the man I was going to marry! *You're* not Dan Marriott. You're Standish. *Ridge Standish!"*

The chair and the floor and the earth itself seemed to teeter and fall violently away.

22

Ginnie's voice hissed and echoed through the phone as if from some astral region . . .

"I first began to wonder about you when I saw you smoking cigarettes. Dan never smoked them—only a pipe. And his pipe had a *straight* stem, not a curved stem like the one on the pipe you found. That had to be someone else's, probably thrown away years ago. There were other things. Dan never called his wife Judith, always Judie. And the way you moved, little mannerisms—they were unlike Dan's. I didn't *really* begin to think about all those things until after that night . . . that night in the kitchen. It was *different*. I can't tell you exactly how or why—but afterwards I began to be sure you were not Dan Marriott. It took a lot of thinking to figure out and convince myself you must be Ridge Standish. It seemed too bizarre."

Suddenly I seemed to be spinning in a world of ectoplasmic shapes. Ginnie's voice faded into the distance, the sound coming through but not the sense. Faces materialized against a black metal backdrop, joined themselves to voices . . .

"Really Ridge! MUST you wear that old jacket!" Patricia my wife. Former wife. Familiarly petulant, whining in complaint. "You know the Whitleys are stopping by. Really Ridge! Really Ridge really Ridge" . . . Her shrew's face dissolved into Jill's lovely sixteen-year-old image, voice soft and grave: "Daddy, I won't go away to that school if you'd rather I stayed." "No, honey, I think it's best you get away." "Are you and mother going to get a divorce?" "Yes, Jill." . . . August Stone pushed forward, toad-shaped but with a darkly attractive face, his hand resting uncomfortably on my shoulder: "If you won't do it for yourself, do it for the firm, Ridge. You're in no state of mind to work effectively. I'm almost ordering you— take a good long vacation." Why did I refuse? Because I questioned his sincerity? . . . Marshall Whitley, wavy white hair setting off his round pink cheeks, said in that voice I'd have chosen for a father's, "I don't always agree with August, Ridge. But this time I do. Get away for a couple of months. As a favor to me." Looking into his wide, compassionate eyes, I nodded . . .

Faces on airplanes, faces in hotel lobbies, faces around swimming pools and bars. One of them, mustached and slightly pompous, emerged vividly only a few feet away. We stood at a bar in Puerto Vallarta. Jeb Scott. And beside him his wife, Ginnie. "I'm Ridge Standish. You must be the friends the Marriotts are meeting. I was with them in Acapulco." Ginnie's face, wanly pretty, sharpened inquisitively. The Marriotts floated in, Dan politely diffident, Judith gorgeous in white, all but ignoring her husband as she swept majestically to a table and signalled

*me to sit next to her. An overlapping picture—days be-
fore, Judith and I walking the beach in Acapulco (Dan
was napping) and stopping at a wild Mexican cantina
where the waiters danced with the tourists. We drank te-
quila, three of them. Judith said, "I suppose you know
our marriage doesn't really exist." Eyes meaningful. "I
mean literally does not exist. Dan's past all that." Shock.
Not simply because of the disloyalty but more because of
the clear implication that Dan Marriott was impotent. He
was about my age—a good looking man, though his features had partially receded into flesh. Was it his impotence
that made him seem more at ease with the seemingly sex-
less Ginnie Scott? Judith: "He treats me like some dim-
witted daughter. Judie, he calls me. JUDIE! I hate that
name!" I was sorry for her—and attracted. That evening,
strolling outside the Whiskey A Go Go to get some air,
suddenly kissing, bodies pasted together, her hips tunnel-
ing into mine. Thinking: If the place was right, I'd take
her now. Later glad the place had not been right. Why
settle on Judith Marriott? There were plenty of attractive
single women . . .*

*The Marriotts' last night in Puerto Vallarta. We said
goodbye, Judith looking at me strangely—there had been
nothing since that kiss—and away they went to their
room. Alone, I took a moonlight dip in the shallow pool,
dried off and lay on a divan. Suddenly there was Judith,
wearing a bikini and clutching two glasses half filled with
scotch. Drinking, talking, smoking. Then she was next
to me. We kissed. She drew back and ripped off her bra.
I sat stunned as she plucked at the strings of the bottoms,*

*finally taking them off. Harshly she said, "Now! It's got
to be now!" The preliminaries were brief. I was on my
back, Judith taking charge, absorbing me into her frenetic body . . .*

*The next morning a note under my door. A plea to stop
in San Francisco on my way back to New York. I shook
my head—oh, no. Days of loneliness. Why not? The marriage no longer really existed, and she was a desirable
woman. Besides, there was a tantalizing urge to be the
aggressor . . . Her delighted surprise when I called from
the Mark Hopkins . . . Day after day at The Hacienda.
(What was the manager's name? Costa.) It was all too
much. I had to get away . . .*

*Friday before New Year's. Judith stormed into my hotel
room. Dan Marriott had found out about us. He wanted
a divorce. Would I stand by her? Marriage! I stalled:
"Maybe it won't come to that. Let's wait and see." I
thought of flying out that night. Somehow I couldn't. I
would at least stay for the weekend, face Marriott myself
if necessary and try to convince him there would be nothing more between his wife and me . . . The next night,
New Year's Eve. Judith and her husband were going to a
party at the Scotts', "for appearances' sake. . . ."*

*The lower bar at the Mark Hopkins. I stood alone,
surrounded by revellers. Drinking, talking to strangers,
postponing the return to that empty room . . . Two A.M.
Enough. I hadn't had a bite to eat since lunch. In my room
I ordered up a sandwich and a glass of milk. I drank the
milk, ate half the sandwich and stretched out on the bed.
Sleep . . .*

But only for a few minutes. The phone screamed through troubled dreams. Judith shrieked, "Ridge, something horrible has happened. Please, please come out and help me!" An accident, she said. Dan was hurt. I listened groggily. I'd turned in my rental car, I had no transportation. "Take a cab. Oh, you've got to help me Ridge, you've got to!" I agreed, too woozy to ask about the accident. She'd pick me up at a bar in Sausalito—Ziggie's—drive me back later. I was still dressed. I got a cab downstairs and was in the Sausalito parking lot at three-twenty. The bar was closed.

Judith beeped her horn as the cab drove away. I slid in beside her. Her tongue darted over trembling lips, her eyes stared. I said I'd drive and we exchanged seats. What had happened? She started to cry. "We had a fight at the party. I left and called you but you weren't there. I went back and drove Dan home. The fight got worse. Terrible. He came at me and I . . ." She stopped, sobbing. "You hit him with something?" "Yes . . . yes . . . that's it. I hit him with . . . something." "Where is he now?" "I left him on the floor of his bedroom." "You mean he's dying!" Silence. "Judith!" "Ridge, I don't know!" . . . I was silent, driving, approaching Kentwood . . .

"Ridge, oh my God, I love you! You've got to stick with me. Ridge! I can say it was self defense, that he tried to kill me. Let him die there. Ridge, let him die!"

"We can't do that."

"Yes, we can! Oh, Ridge, I can get out of this. Then there'll be just you and me. There's a lot of money, Ridge. We can have it all. Just us. A lot of money. Oh, God, I love you, Ridge. We can be married and have it all."

"*No!*"

She coiled back into the corner of the seat. We both lit cigarettes. Clouds of smoke billowed and danced in the green glow of the instrument pane.

I said nothing until we started up the hill leading to her house.

"*Judith, you have to face the truth. We can never be married. If I can get a plane, I'm leaving for New York this afternoon.*"

A deadly silence. Then suddenly she sprang at me, fists pummeling my shoulder.

"*You dirty son of a bitch!*"

I warded her off with my right forearm, dropping my cigarette to push her back. She hustled back at me like an enraged beast bursting from its cage. Clawing, scratching, biting. Panting obscenities.

"*Goddam it, Judith! Stop! Now!*"

She gouged at my eyes. I reached my foot for the brake but her leg slammed over mine as if for leverage. My foot was locked on the accelerator. Her whole weight was on it as she clawed at my face. I felt the car leap forward. I twisted and the steering wheel spun from one hand. There was a heart gasping skid. We struck the shoulder of the road and careened over it. For an instant we seemed airborne.

"*JUDITH! MY GOD!*"

We struck. Her door sprang open. The car, somersaulting, plummetted down down down . . .

"Are you there?"

It was Ginnie Scott's voice, seeming to come from my

hip. I was sitting flat on the floor propped against the chair, my hand gripping the phone next to my thigh. I picked up the phone—it felt like a ton—and pushed it against my ear.

"Yes, I'm here. But I'll have to talk to you later. I've got to"—I was about to say "get sick" but instead finished weakly, "got to get used to this."

With a great effort, I reached and hung up the phone. Staggering to my feet, head held low, I shook myself to the kitchen and gulped vodka straight from the bottle. I spit up some in the sink, then took another. I stood there gripping the cold tile.

Ridge Standish. *I* was Ridge Standish. Everything that had whirled through my mind was true. Memory had come back. There were still dark pockets of forgetfulness—details—but the essentials were clear.

I was Ridge Standish but the face was Dan Marriott's. How had that been accomplished and why? No matter now. Later. First a mirror. I had tried to ignore the face I wore. Now I was driven by compulsion to see it, inspect it carefully, try to imagine my own beneath it.

The drinks were working. I dashed up the stairs to my room, I stood in front of the full length mirror on my side of the bathroom door. I pushed my face up close, rubbing my hands over the almost invisible scars and seams. The face meant nothing to me. It was still Dan Marriott's.

I looked deep into the eyes. Miraculously, in imagination, the face was replaced by my own. It was not too unlike Dan Marriott's. Same broad forehead, same high cheekbones, same short nose. But where Marriott's had been fleshy, mine was lean and taut. More like Marriott, perhaps, as he had been years ago.

The face seemed to recede in the mirror as though I were backing away. But I was standing rigidly still. I seemed to be looking into some sort of trick mirror that reflected different images. Now I saw myself at an angle. Then I realized . . .

The door opened wide. On the other side, standing in the bathroom, was a woman in a black dress with blonde hair piled high. In her hand, steady as steel, glittered a gun pointed straight at my belly.

23

My heart did a flipflop. I stared at the gun, backed up a step and raised my eyes. It took a moment to comprehend that the heavily mascaraed and lipsticked face beneath the stack of blonde hair was Judith's.

I gulped out, "How did you get here?"

"Through the back door. I *did* keep my key."

So perhaps it was not a deer or raccoon I had heard. "I mean, you're supposed to be in Los Angeles."

She gave me a cold, smug smile. "Just as I thought—I *was* being followed. Now it's exactly as I want it—I'm supposed to be in Los Angeles." She patted the blonde hair, a wig. "The planes fly up to San Francisco every few minutes, you know." She waved the gun toward the bedroom door. "Stand over there next to the wall."

I obeyed. "Judith, you don't have a chance in the world."

Her lip curved scornfully. "It's you who've run out of chances." She pushed the gun forward. "First I want those film strips. You'll give them to me or I'll shoot you dead."

"I don't have them."

"That's a lie."

"I couldn't get them now if I wanted to. They're in Gus Klein's safe."

Her eyes wavered: She believed me. "Stupid! He could have blackmailed you."

"I trusted Gus Klein."

She shook her head, bouncing the blonde wig. "It doesn't matter. That was a long time ago. The pictures can't really hurt me now."

She moved back and sat on the bed, holding the gun level. I braced against the wall as if facing a firing squad.

She looked at me stonily. "I'm going to kill you. I guess you know that."

I sucked in a breath. "Why do you want to kill me?"

"That should be obvious. For one thing, as your widow I'll be a fairly rich woman."

I was astounded. Was she mad enough to believe she could get away with killing me when the police already suspected her of killing Gus Klein and possessed proof she had murdered a man they thought was Standish?

"You'll never collect, Judith. You're wanted for murder right this minute."

She sneered. "Gus Klein? The police haven't a speck of evidence against me on that. If they did, they wouldn't have just *followed* me. They'd have arrested me."

So she had not heard the news bulletin reporting the second murder. She had already entered the house and gone upstairs when the announcer had interrupted the TV western.

"I'm not talking about Gus Klein, Judith."

Her gun hand jerked. "What *are* you talking about?"

I felt an aftershock, remembering where Ginnie had said the second body was found. Her words had been lost in the kaleidoscope of returning memory.

"I'm talking about the body the police dug up a short time ago. The body you buried under the same abandoned ship where they found Gus Klein."

Her face drained. The gun shook.

"The body of the man you murdered early last New Year's Day. Your husband—*Dan Marriott.*"

For an instant she did not move. Then slowly, like a pneumatic toy deflating, she crumpled. Her mouth went slack, her shoulders sagged, the gun dropped to her knee.

She started to speak in a dry whisper: "Then . . ."

"I know that I'm Ridge Standish." There was no sense in telling her of the police's confusion; they would find out which man was which soon enough. "There was a news report about the body found buried in the ship. It said the police know the killer."

She looked almost listlessly at the gun as though not comprehending what it was. I took one step forward. She stiffened and raised the gun. I stopped.

She spoke in a faraway voice. "Then it was the police you kept talking to on the phone. I was afraid you'd shout for help if I came down."

Softly I said, "It's all over now, Judith. Give me the gun."

"No!" Limply she waved it at me. Then she pointed it at the center of the rug. "Dan stood there when I shot him. It was a nasty, nasty fight. I guess I wanted him dead ever since I met you, Ridge. Maybe before. But I don't even remember taking the gun out of the desk drawer."

I forced my voice to a normal tone. "Was he dead when you called me at the hotel?"

"No. But he was when I hung up and came back to this room. He'd moved while I was out. I guess he had just enough life left to get up and hide the film strip in the humidor."

"Did you *ever* tell me he was dead?"

"No. And for the same reason I didn't tell you about the Hacienda pictures: I was afraid you'd run out. I thought I'd better break the news slowly. I hoped when I asked you to meet me in Sausalito that you might see it through with me . . . later on, marry me. Then I could have stood up to the police. I'd have said Dan abused me—we *did* have separate rooms—and that he attacked me and I was terrified and killed him to protect myself. I was even going to say he was having an affair with another woman."

And the police, I thought, would have found out it was true.

"If the police believed Dan had been seeing another woman, they might not judge me too harshly if they found the film strip." She gave a long shuddering sigh. "I think it would have worked. But *you*—you wouldn't cooperate, Ridge. You didn't give a goddam about me and as much as told me so."

"I remember, Judith. You fought me in the car."

She looked at me curiously. "When did you start to remember, Ridge?"

"Only this evening. After I heard they'd found Dan's body. That meant I had to be Ridge Standish. Then everything began coming back."

She bit her lip. "I thought it was you who telephoned, who sent the telegram, who asked that I look up Shelley's poem. I remembered one day seeing you looking at our copy of Palgrave."

"No, I wasn't the one. It . . ." I shut my mouth. Nothing could be gained by telling her it was Ginnie.

"Then it had to be Gus Klein. But you must have known what he was doing. It had me terribly worried. I went down to the boat a few days ago. I wanted to make sure no one had found . . . where Dan was. The next time I went there, yesterday, I knew I'd be followed. But I thought it would be you. I thought it was you in the front of the boat." She closed her eyes as though hypnotized. "I planned to wait until dark, then bury you under that junk on the causeway they're forever building. They'd be dumping more and more junk on top of it and you'd never be found."

My voice gravelled through my dry throat. "Was that your plan for tonight?"

She gave a crestfallen nod, looking like a child who has failed at some simple task. "I was going to force you to drive your Porsche down there and shoot you. Then bury you in the causeway. I'd drive the car to the Golden Gate Bridge and leave it there. Then I'd fly back to my motel in Los Angeles. I'd be there in less than two hours. My car was in the garage under my room. I'd told the switchboard operator late this afternoon that I wasn't to be disturbed as I'd been driving all day. I'd get rid of this wig I bought and it would look like I'd never left. Meanwhile the police would have found your empty Porsche with your jacket inside and your wallet, and maybe think you'd jumped off the Bridge in despair. Or maybe faked it and gone away, the way people with amnesia often do. I remembered the doctors at the clinic saying it happens all the time. Especially in what they called the fugue state, the term they used to describe *your* condition. The police would have found that out and, I think, given up."

She had calculated with the reckless cunning of a psychopath. Could her mind have cracked?

I said, knowing the answer, "Why didn't you bury Gus Klein in the causeway?"

"Because I heard a noise, like a foot snapping a piece of wood. I ran. On the way home, I thought it might have been somone just idly passing by. I was going to go back later. But then, just before you got home, I heard on the news that the police had found Klein's body. I didn't think they could tie me to it. I'd been very careful."

"Weren't you worried about the other body—Dan's?"

"Worried, yes. But there was no mention of it on the news. And neither you nor the police tried to stop me when I left here last night. So I told myself that no one even suspected another body. And if that was true, you must believe that Standish—the man you assumed was Standish—was still alive. Therefore, you'd think *he* was the one who killed Gus Klein, perhaps suspecting me as an accomplice but unable to prove it. The police would go on chasing a ghost, the wrong ghost, until finally they'd quit."

"If you believed that, why didn't you just stay at home and brazen it out?"

She stared at the barrel of the gun, as if not hearing. Then: "Because, even with your amnesia, I no longer trusted you. And I knew there would come a day when you'd remember everything. You'd remember that I was responsible for the car going off the road, almost killing you. There was a chance—that's what I'd hoped for—a chance that if you'd come to love me deeply, you'd have a way to rationalize all that and learn to accept it. That didn't happen. You didn't want me when you were Ridge Standish and you didn't want me when you still thought you were Dan Marriott. Eventually you'd have handed me over to the police. I had no choice. I had to kill you. And if it worked out as I planned, I'd be a rich widow." She sagged on the bed. "But, as you see, it didn't work out."

Finally I asked the question that had been gnawing at my mind ever since Ginnie revealed my true identity.

"How . . . why . . . did you get the insane idea to transform me into your husband?"

Almost wistfully she studied my face. "I've already told you part of that. Because I wanted you. I never in my life wanted a man the way I wanted you." Her voice became matter of fact. "And look at the position we were in. I had picked up Dan at the Scotts' party at two A.M. to drive him home. Jeb *saw* me pick him up. We got home before two-thirty and a little while later Dan was dead. You came out and we smashed up shortly after three-thirty. What would it have looked like with Dan shot to death and you and I together in an accident? Like Judith Marriott and her lover Ridge Standish—and they could prove you were my lover with those pictures—had deliberately conspired to murder Dan Marriott. The self-defense argument would be demolished. Then we'd *both* get it—at least life."

I saw now that if I *had* loved her, I might have sympathized with her dilemma and remained forever silent. I might even have talked myself into being wryly grateful, for even though she had, in her rage, instigated the accident, she had helped to save my life afterwards and protected me against a charge of conspiring to commit murder.

"I had no alternative. I had to conceal Dan's death and I had to avoid any suspicion that you and I were together. There was only one answer: turn you into Dan. The idea didn't come to me right away. Certainly not when I was at the bottom of the mountain swabbing your face. God, that face—there seemed to be nothing left of it. After I went up to the house to call for help, I was frantic about what to do. I rushed upstairs. I looked at Dan lying there dead and almost went out of my mind. I ran down to the kitchen and gulped a big drink of whiskey. I brought another one into the living room and stood there staring at the telephone in the hall. It was hopeless, I told myself. I'd just have to give myself up and see if a good lawyer could keep me out of the gas chamber. Then I turned around, looking at the mantel, and saw Dan's and my pictures in the matching frames, the ones you had at the clinic. They'd been taken seven or eight years ago, when Dan was a lot thinner. I thought how remarkably he resembled you. He was your height, was then about the same weight, had the same color eyes and hair and similar features. You could have been brothers. I don't wonder I found him attractive in those days. The idea started slowly, then came in a big flash as I thought of your crushed face. I dashed upstairs and emptied Dan's pockets. That's when I found the pictures, in his wallet, and burned them. I got his body zippered into a sleeping bag and locked it in the storage closet. *Then* I called the police. It was four-thirty. I jumped into the Porsche, drove back to you, emptied *your* pockets, put everything into my handbag and substituted Dan's things. I finished just as the police arrived on the road. They had no reason to believe you were anyone but my husband."

I hunched back against the wall, overwhelmingly tired. "What if I had died?"

"They'd have thought it was Dan. The condition of the body would have made it unidentifiable unless somebody really wanted to probe. And why should they? Dan and I had been seen together at the party. We'd been seen leaving together. There was only the time discrepancy to account for. And I think I satisfied the police that I'd been unconscious."

She had not satisfied Sheriff Bogano but that was academic now.

"I'd still have buried Dan where I did and no one would ever have known. I'd be alone but I'd have a lot of money for company."

In a dead voice that had gone far beyond caring, she told me the rest of it. Two nights later, having driven around looking for a desolate location, she crammed Dan's bagged body into the trunk of the Porsche and hauled it down beside the ancient boat. At first she had dug only a shallow grave in the muddy dirt floor of the bottomless bow. But, as the weeks passed, she visited there frequently, each time deepening the hole and packing the earth tighter. Finally she left it with only a dank puddle as a marker. Meanwhile I had emerged from coma conveniently amnesic, and she shipped me in an ambulance to the clinic outside of Santa Barbara. ("Dr. Stryker, I knew, was one of the best plastic surgeons in the country. Besides, I wanted to get away from people Dan knew. Especially the Scotts, and any snooping policemen.") She gave the doctor Dan Marriott's portrait, along with a batch of snapshots taken at about the same time, as guides for the plastically-molded result.

Now she looked intently into my face. Her mouth, thick with lipstick, curled into a bitter smile. "It would never have worked anyway, Ridge. You began to remind me too much of *him*. I found I was *glad* when you moved into this room. Everything was breaking down all over again, just as it had with Dan."

Her head snapped up. In the distance we heard the eerie wail of sirens.

Judith jumped to her feet. I started toward her, holding out my hand for the gun.

She backed off a step, shot out her arm and pointed the gun at my chest. "Stop right there, Ridge!"

I was startled. I thought she had continued to retain the weapon only as a mock deterrent while she unburdened herself. Could she possibly think there was a chance for her?

"Judith, they've got Dan's body. They've got the bullet that matches that gun. They've got you trapped here. Give it up."

Her beaded lashes dropped half over speculative eyes. "There's still a way out. Get over in that corner."

I sidled to the corner. Still pointing the gun, she circled to the bedroom door. She yanked it open and darted into the hall. The door slammed shut. I heard the rasp of the key. I stood there for a moment listening to her feet clatter down the stairs. The sirens now wailed in a vast piercing chorus. There was the sound of wheels crunching up the driveway, cars slamming to a stop.

I raced through the bathroom to Judith's room. The door to the hall was unlocked. I flung it wide and lunged through. The door chimes were ringing frantically. A shot from downstairs stopped me dead. The police must have blown the lock. Immediately there was the thud of a body against the front door. It burst open as I sailed off the last step into the hall. Bogano, gun drawn, charged in followed by two uniformed men, both armed.

Judith was nowhere in sight.

"She ran out," I said. "The car!"

"We've got men posted there," Bogano said.

The other policemen had split, one dashing to the kitchen, the other to the dark terrace. Bogano jogged to the terrace, joining the policeman on the coping at the shallow end. I followed, snapping the wall switch for the pool lights.

As I stepped out on the flagstones, I saw it. A widening stain curving through the illuminated blue water as though a giant squid had released its fluid. It was blood.

My eyes followed the trail to where it thickened at its source in the deep end of the pool under the diving board. I heard myself gasp. There, undulating almost perpendicularly against the pool light, black hair floating into the suction of the top drain, was the body of Judith. I knew then that the shot I had heard had nothing to do with a door lock. Half her head had been blow away. She must have held the muzzle to the roof of her mouth.

24

Fifteen minutes later I was alone with Bogano in his car, on the way to his office to answer questions for the official report. Judith's body had been fished from the pool and, when I left, lay supine in its bloody drippings surrounded by milling police officers.

Gripping the wheel, Bogano stared grimly at the descending black road, not speaking until we reached the bottom.

"Mr. Marri—, *Standish,* this might not seem at all important to you now, but it will later. About an hour after you left my office, Marshall Whitley called me back. It was about August Stone. They'd finally got him to explain what happened to the forty thousand dollars that couldn't be accounted for. It seems that the respectable Mr. Stone—a married man—had been keeping a woman. He'd set her up in one of those cooperative apartments on New York's East Side. An apartment that cost exactly forty thousand dollars. So it looks like, legally, you're clean as a priest."

He was right—it didn't seem at all important now. "Fine," I said. I waited a moment and said, "I've begun to remember everything."

Bogano made a whistling sound through his teeth. "Congratulations. I'm glad something good's come out of this mess."

I gazed stuporously at the smoke curling from my cigarette. "Why didn't you call me and tell me about August Stone?"

"Because at that point I didn't know you were Standish." His big hat shook and he gave a low growl. "The body that was dug up in the boat—there was no way of knowing it was Marriott, or anybody. Just bones, hair and some teeth. And the bullet. Which made us think it was Standish. *You,* that is. We wouldn't have had a damned thing if some smart guy in homicide hadn't started wondering if maybe Gus Klein wasn't in there looking for something besides Judith Marriott. He started digging around and—jackpot."

"But if you still thought I was Dan Marriott, what made you come roaring up to the house? You believed Judith was in Los Angeles. With Standish dead, or so you thought, and Judith down there, why would you think I was in any danger?"

"In a way, Mr. Standish, you can thank Gus Klein again for that."

"Gus Klein?"

"The bug. He planted it on your phone. Maybe half an hour ago, the guy monitoring it rushed into my office with a tape. It was the conversation you'd had with Mrs. Scott, when she told you that you were Ridge Standish. Klein seems to have been your guardian angel."

No, this time it had been Ginnie who had saved my life. If she had not told me about the police finding Dan Marriott's body—enabling me to tell it to Judith and thus thwart her last hope for immunity—I would now be a dead man.

I said as much to Bogano, adding, "But I don't understand why Ginnie Scott didn't call the police instead of calling me."

Bogano snorted softly, as though in self-disgust. "She *did* call me—*after* she talked to you. I got the message when I was over in the lab with the coroner checking on Marriott's remains. I said I'd call back. I didn't because by the time I got to my office, we had the tape of her conversation with you. That got me cracking. Among other things, it told me that Judith Marriott had not taken off for Los Angeles with the idea of meeting Standish. I had a sneaky feeling she might be pulling a fast one and come gunning for you."

"I don't know why Ginnie Scott called me at all. She knew I'd been up here seeing Judith just before the accident. She'd been acting cool toward me. She must have been thinking I had something to do with Dan Marriott's death. So why call me and tell me I was Standish, as if to protect me?"

Bogano shot me a surprised glance. "Mr. Standish, she finally figured out that you were just a scapegoat. She was sure that the body we dug up was Marriott's and she knew from the news announcement he'd been killed by a bullet. Chances were it was fired by his wife; after all, *you* had an alibi—the restaurant check you signed showed you were in your hotel room at the time the murder should logically have taken place. She pretty much guessed the rest. It's all on the tape we took off the phone. You must have forgotten. And, believe me, I can't blame you."

So that was what Ginnie had been talking about while I was being besieged by images from the past.

"When she called," Bogano said, "she thought Mrs. Marriott was there in the house with you. She was afraid you might be next on the list. But then you told her Judith Marriott was in Los Angeles. That probably relieved her."

"I'm afraid it's all pretty vague."

"It gets me that this whole crazy case could have been cracked easily even before we found Marriott. You remember the fingerprints we lifted from the boat? Except for Klein's, the only ones we found were Standish's. Well, it would have been the easiest thing in the world for me to have gotten your prints and compared them. We'd have known immediately that you were Standish and that Dan Marriott had disappeared and probably was murdered. I'd have radioed the men following Judith Marriott and right now she'd be in a nice safe jail." Bogano shrugged philosophically. "I don't blame myself too much. Who'd ever suspect anything cockeyed as that you might be Ridge Standish?"

"Ginnie Scott did," I said.

"Yes, but she had something to go on." He cocked an eye at me. "You haven't forgotten how she came to decide that you were Ridge Standish?"

I had, but I started to remember.

Bogano said, "I understand the business about your calling Mrs. Marriott Judith instead of Judie, the cigarettes instead of the pipe, the different mannerisms, all that. But I don't get what she meant about something happening between you two in the kitchen. Do you remember anything about that, Mr. Standish?"

I felt my neck grow hot. "No, not exactly. I guess it must have been the way I . . . reacted to something."

We were driving down the main street. A movie was just letting out. I gawked at the throngs passing the gleaming store windows under the glow of the street lamps. I felt no more a part of them, a part of anything, than if I had just arrived from another planet.

"It's Gus Klein's funeral tomorrow," Bogano said. "You planning to be there?"

"Yes," I said without thinking.

"Good. I'll be there, a couple of cops he used to know on the force, a few from his office. Gus had no family so it doesn't matter that he was broke. His sister died some years ago."

Gus Klein. A solitary man, as I was now. A man who seemed to accept the world as it was but fought back against its melancholy challenges. I had not even paid him. I would arrange somehow to take care of the funeral expenses.

At least I was alive. I rubbed my hands over the stitched face that would forever be a stranger to me. I was aware of the rhythmic beat of my heart. *My* heart, Ridge Standish's. I had the sudden belief that it held all that was needed of courage and compassion and, above all, hope.

About the Author

Richard Neely started out as a New York City newspaperman. He also worked as an advertising executive before becoming a full-time writer. He is the author of 15 novels, including *The Walter Syndrome*, and currently lives with his wife in Marin County, California.